CANE'S BREAK

BY PATRICK HENNESSY

2/17/2016

to Rebecca

enjoy this

Pat

Copyright © 2015 by Patrick Hennessy

ISBN 978-1-519672-76-6

All rights reserved. This book or any portion thereof may not be reproduced or used in any manner whatsoever without the express written permission of the publisher except for the use of brief quotations in a book review.

Cover design by Danielle Fauber of Kalmbach Smith Meadows, 1530 Fairfield Avenue, Shreveport, LA 71101 | goksm.com

Painting By: Julie Miller

FORWARD

I created the characters and the story. I made up the people in this story; they do not exist in real life. Most of the places do exist, but probably not exactly as described.

While this book is not about country music, it is filled with many of country music's themes.

The songs I used do exist and with one exception the artists have a strong connection with Northwest Louisiana. The connection is usually the Louisiana Hayride which was performed at the Municipal Auditorium in Shreveport from 1948 to 1960. The Hayride was broadcast on radio station KWKH, as well as many other stations and even the CBS radio network. Many stars got their start on the Hayride "The Cradle of the Stars" including: Webb Pierce, Hank Williams, Elvis, Johnny Cash, Faron Young, Jim Reeves, George Jones, James Burton, David Houston, and Johnny Horton.

The songs I used as chapter titles have something to do with the contents of the chapter they head. That connection may sometimes be lost to the reader, but in some instances the reader may find a connection I never consciously intended. By way of introduction and background, I have listed the chapter titles and artists below.

The flamboyant Webb Pierce was an early performer on the Hayride. Recordings by Webb Pierce used as chapter headings are: *Wondering*; and, *Pick Me up on Your Way Down*. Webb Pierce was inducted into the Country Music Hall of Fame in 2001.

The incomparable Hank Williams first appeared on the Hayride in April of 1948. Songs by Hank Williams used in this book as chapter headings are: *Hey Good Lookin', I Saw the Light, Mind Your Own Business, I'll Never Get Out of This World Alive, I Can't Help I (If I'm Still in Love With You), Setting the Woods on Fire,* and *Lost Highway*. My parents never played country music in our house or in the car. My first memory of a Hank William's song was one of my high school teachers standing in the door way to the class room singing *Long Gone Lonesome Blues*. That song did not make it into this book nor did many of Hank's other remarkable songs, but if you listen to music, at all, you will probably hear one of his songs before the week is out.

Hank Williams, Jr. was born in Shreveport, Louisiana, on May 26, 1949 less than a year after his father made his first appearance on the Hayride. *Whiskey Bent and Hell Bound* and *Family Tradition* seemed apt titles to chapters of this book.

Like Hank Jr., Joe Stampley is a little young to have appeared on the Hayride, but he was born sixty miles from Shreveport in Springhill, Louisiana. One of his hits was used: *Roll on Big Mama*.

I don't know if Sonny James performed *Young Love* at the Hayride though he did perform there. *Young Love* was released in 1954.

Jim Reeves started out on the Hayride as an announcer and became one of the all-time greats. If *Am I that Easy to Forget* doesn't get you, surely *Welcome To My World* will.

Claude King lived most of his life in Shreveport, Louisiana. There are no mountains in Shreveport or anywhere in Louisiana, but King made a huge hit about a mountain, *Wolverton Mountain,* from a song written by Merle Kilgore who also grew up in Shreveport.

The artist without a strong connection to north Louisiana, David Alan Coe, has appeared many times in Shreveport and the song used in this story, *The Ride,* is about Hank Williams.

George Jones was on the Hayride at the same time as were Johnny Cash and Elvis. Some think that *He Stopped Loving Her Today* is the greatest country song ever recorded.

Jean Sheppard was a country star and a performer on the Hayride. She had a big hit with *I'll Take the Dog,* a duet she recorded with Ray Pillow.

Johnny Cash was another star who got a break on the Hayride. Two of his songs were used *Folsom Prison Blues* and the less familiar, but appropriate heading for the chapter titled, *Rough Neck.*

Few consider Elvis to have been a country singer, but most know that he got his first big break on the Hayride, so *Jailhouse Rock* was included as a chapter title.

Faron Young was born in Shreveport and graduated from Fair Park High School, in Shreveport. Faron started on the Hayride and eventually had five number one hits. Three were used, *Hello Walls,* my favorite, written by Willie Nelson' *Live Fast, Love Hard, Die Young,* and, *It's Four in the Morning.*

The version of Suzie-Q referenced here is the original by Dale Hawkins with James Burton on guitar. James Burton reportedly composed the guitar licks for *Suzie-Q* when he was fourteen. Both men appeared on the Hayride.

David Houston was from Bossier City and was in some ways the inspiration for this book. In 1964, I heard a teacher criticize David Houston for wasting his beautiful voice on country music. From that day forward my guilty pleasure has been country music. *Almost Persuaded* was number one on the country charts for nine straight weeks. It is one of the biggest country hits of all time and it's not about cheating or lonesome lost love.

Kitty Wells was an early female star. Her song is a classic, *It Wasn't God Who Made Honky Tonk Angels.*

Nat Stuckey seems to be an underappreciated Hayride star. It is hard to believe that *Don't Pay the Ransom* never made it to number one nor did *Pop a Top Again,* which he also wrote and recorded, not even when later recorded by Jim Ed Brown nor even later when recorded by Alan Jackson.

While some historians dispute the fact that Jimmie Davis actually wrote *You Are My Sunshine,* he gets credit for the song which is without doubt one of the most popular country songs of all time. Davis appeared on the Hayride, lived on Delaware Street in Shreveport and was at one time Shreveport's Public Service Commissioner. Davis later served two terms as governor of Louisiana.

In mid-50's Johnny Horton lived two doors down from me on Rodney Street in Bossier City, Louisiana. He was married to Hank William's widow Billie Jean. By the end of 1960, Johnny Horton had released three number one hits including *The Battle of New Orleans* and would die in a car wreck caused by a drunk driver. I had to include at least one Johnny Horton song as a chapter heading.

All of the songs can be found and enjoyed on YouTube. I have checked and have included current links. You may want to listen to the songs before, during or after reading a chapter.

CHAPTER 1 - *WONDERING.*
Webb Pierce
https://www.youtube.com/watch?v=hHGjYhSKeWQ

Jake was thinking that his life was not turning out anything like he had planned while fully realizing that he had not actually planned anything.

It was an unseasonably cool late August morning. Rain was coming. Jake had been driving for over 10 hours. To stay awake, he was listening to the radio, turned up too loud, drinking cokes and had detoured off of the interstate highway. He was now stopped at a used car lot near Brownsville, Tennessee, using a hedge of waxy leaf ligustrums as an outdoor urinal...the cool air would have helped had he needed any.

The long trip had given him time to think. And right now, he was thinking that he should have taken a plane or, better yet, sent his son off to college on a plane and stayed home.

There was no traffic on the outskirts of Brownsville at 1:30 in the morning. It was cloudy, moonless, dark and still. The only light came from the few, scattered, worn-out flood lights in the car lot. Jake's pearl white Ford Police Interceptor was undoubtedly the most valuable car in that lot. The only sounds were the sawing of crickets and the croaking of tree frogs in some distant trees.

Jake's pity party was abruptly interrupted by the appearance of a shiny black Cadillac Escalade that quietly turned into an empty, unlit lot adjacent to where Jake stood. Something told Jake that he should stay still and invisible, if possible. Within a minute a second vehicle, a black Tahoe, came from the west and also turned into the now occupied lot. The tires of the truck kicked up dust and made crunching sounds in the gravel lot as the Tahoe came to a stop.

Jake shifted further into the ligustrum hedge and silently watched. He was probably 50 yards away, but his eyes were accustomed to the darkness and he could see two men emerge from each vehicle. One of the men from the Cadillac was carrying a large black suitcase with rollers. When a third man appeared from the Tahoe with an aluminum briefcase, Jake knew he best stay in the shadows of the hedge, out of sight.

All five men wore dark clothes, a couple wore black bomber jackets or maybe they were biker jackets. Two of the men began to talk. The others stood facing each other but said nothing. Jake was a little too far away to hear what was being said. But the body language and the tension rolling off the members of the group was enough to keep Jake from taking any chances. The voices of the two who were talking grew louder. Jake could now hear curse words flying back and forth. Each group turned slightly as if to return to their vehicles, but no one fully turned their back and none of them took their eyes off the others.

Then, with no warning and for no reason Jake could discern, one of the men drew a gun from his black leather coat and began shooting. It happened so fast that Jake could not tell who started shooting first. Within an instant, both groups of men had guns drawn and were shooting at each other. Jake heard bullets hitting the ligustrum as they zipped by his head. Jake had no law enforcement or military training, but he hit the ground like someone who did. Within seconds the shooting ceased and there was total silence. Even the crickets and frogs were quiet. There was no sound, only darkness and silence.

Jake lay still, hugging the ground, barely breathing, afraid to move. Jake had never been so frightened, not even when his wife had threatened to shoot him with his shotgun. There was nothing but darkness and silence. Jake could hear himself breathing... a good thing he thought.

Gradually, the crickets and frogs resumed their concert. Jake realized he could not lie there hugging the ground forever.

Jake had made a lot of good decisions in his 43 years... and one particularly bad one. He was about to make, what most would consider, a particularly bad decision. A decision that would change his already messed up life for the worst. God knows, it was a decision that James 'Jake' Caldwell Cane would not have even considered two years ago.

Jake slowly rose from his prone position and stayed as quiet as possible within the false security of the hedge. He saw no movement as he peered through the branches. Jake eased from his hiding place.

Nothing and no one moved. Somehow drawn, but literally shaking, Jake stepped from his hiding place and carefully inched toward the lot where the men lay unnaturally still, always staying as close as possible to the hedge. Eventually, he was forced into the open. Still no movement and no sound from the men, only the smell of gunpowder mixed with the smell of the rain about to fall. Jake could now see all five men lying awkwardly about the lot.

Jake had never seen a dead man except at funerals which he avoided if possible. These men all looked dead. Jake was not about to feel for a pulse like they do in movies, he didn't want to touch anyone or anything.

Two years ago Jake would have simply grabbed his cell phone from his car and called 911. Jake should have retrieved his cell phone and called 911 and he might have, had he not left the phone in the car, more than 50 yards away.

Sometimes the mind just doesn't work right. While he should have been going for his cell phone,

Jake instead began to focus on the two cases now lying unattended among the mayhem.

Those cases contained something valuable... valuable enough to kill and die for, probably money and drugs. A bird's nest on the ground. These men no longer needed whatever was in those cases. So Jake took them, picked one up in each hand and ran to his car. As he ran away he thought he heard a sound, a moan from the lot, but he didn't turn around to look and he didn't slow down. When he arrived at the car, Jake threw in the cases, started the engine, took a deep breath and slowly drove away.

As he left the car lot, the rain started to fall and was almost immediately a Tennessee downpour. Jake could barely see past the front of his car. He did not look back. Had he looked back, he might have seen that one of the men lying in the cool, now muddy lot was actually alive and that the man was watching Jake as he drove away.

Jake's car radio was on, tuned into KWKH, a station out of Jake's hometown, Shreveport, Louisiana; turned up a little too loud. As he drove west out of

Brownsville, the sound of Webb Pierce came yodeling from the speakers: *Wondering.* Jake's thoughts turn to his wife.

"...Wondering if you're wondering too?"

He should have called 911. He should have turned around. He should have put the cases back where he found them.

Instead, he kept driving, looking for the first road that would take him back to I-40.

CHAPTER 2 - *WHISKEY BENT AND HELL BOUND.* Hank Williams, Jr.
https://www.youtube.com/watch?v=u2V4UUjYBsA

Jake was born at the now demolished P & S Hospital on Line Ave at Jordan in Shreveport, Louisiana. He was from an old, established Shreveport family of farmers, bankers, and oilmen. Jake was the youngest of three children, the caboose, and a real surprise to his forty-year-old parents. Jake's ancestors were among the earliest settlers of Bossier Parish, just across the Red River from Shreveport. When Jake was born, Bossier City was considered to be a hick town inhabited by what Shreveporters called River Rats. Prominent citizens of Shreveport didn't frequent Bossier City or, at least, they didn't admit to their visits to the many strip clubs and bars lining the 'Bossier Strip'. Jake's father, John Stockwell Cane III was the president of Cane Oil & Gas Company, an oil and gas operating company started by Jake's grandfather. The company had been hugely successful after World War II but fell on hard times under the leadership of Jake's father. Jake's father could never quite live up to the legend of Jake's grandfather and by the time Jake entered high school his father had given up, spending most of his days at the Elks Club downtown drinking and playing cards, and most of his nights at The Cub, a bar so old that even Jake's grandfather had been a patron on occasions.

John Cane was a drunken womanizer with a poor reputation in the oil and gas industry. As is often the case with people such as John Cane, he simply could not be trusted in life or in business. Eventually, the family's memberships at The Shreveport Country Club and at the Shreveport Club were being paid by Jake's maternal grandparents, as was Jake's tuition to the prestigious Southfield School. With help from his mother's parents and the dwindling royalties from his grandfather's successful wells, Jake was able to grow up in Shreveport's society, attend Byrd High School and graduate with grades good enough to get him into LSU in Baton Rouge. In spite of all else, John Cane loved his only son and took him hunting and fishing. John Cane reserved most, if not all of his love and time, for his son and Jake truly loved his father.

While in high school, Jake played on the football team as a backup safety and was a member of the student council. He never really liked playing football. He didn't like being hit, which was fine because he had neither the size and the speed, nor the toughness to be much of a football player. Jake also played baseball with even less success; he could hit a fastball, but he couldn't hit a curve and had a mediocre arm.

Unfortunately, when Jake was in his last year at LSU in Baton Rouge, his father was found stabbed to death at a motel on the Bossier Strip. No one talked about the incident in polite company but the rumors around town suggested everything from an unpaid gambling debt, to a liaison with a whore gone wrong and even to an encounter with a spurned homosexual lover. A cheated business associate could have been involved as well. The crime was never solved. Jake loved his father, but he knew his father better than anyone and Jake was not stupid. The financial conditions of Cane Oil & Gas did not surprise him, but the rumors did; and they hurt, causing him to never again fully trust Shreveport society.

Jake's much older sisters had married and long since left Shreveport, one for Dallas, and the other for Houston, so it was up to him to return to Shreveport to take over the family business. Thankfully, Jake did have one unfailing asset- his mother, Eloise Caldwell Cane, a true, Southern lady and the rock that shaped him and allowed him to deal with the death of his father and the attendant burdens forced upon his shoulders.

The Jake Cane, who returned to Shreveport to take over the family business, was immature, but well respected for good reason. He had none of his father's foibles; he was personable, trustworthy ,and reasonably good looking, with light brown hair, blue eyes and a strong even chiseled jaw.

At five foot ten and about one hundred and seventy pounds, Jake had an air of confidence and a gift for conversation. He never drank to excess, he didn't gamble—unless wagers on the golf course count as gambling, and he regularly attended the Methodist Church at the head of Texas Street, played golf reasonably well at the Shreveport Country Club, did not hang around The Cub or the Elks Club, and he never frequented the bars on the Bossier Strip.

Most importantly, he was a Cane. The son of Eloise Caldwell, and as such, he knew everyone who was anyone and *they* knew him. The future looked bright for young James 'Jake' Caldwell Cane when he returned to Shreveport some 20 years ago.

As a young man Jake's father had frequently attended the Louisiana Hayride. John Cane knew of Hank Williams, Sr. John often told his son about seeing Hank Sr. perform, and he could remember when Hank Jr. was born in Shreveport.

Jake knew his father shared Hank Williams' interest in hard liquor and country music, and he also knew John and Hank Sr. shared the fact that they were good men when sober—although neither was sober often enough. John passed on his love of country music to his son. Jake would often fantasize that Hank Jr. was thinking about Jake's father when he wrote *Whiskey Bent and Hell Bound*.

CHAPTER 3 - *ROLL ON BIG MAMA.*
Joe Stampley & Moe Bandy
https://www.youtube.com/watch?v=KsPJt7X9r_8

The pouring rain didn't bother Jake as he drove west on US 79. If you grow up in Louisiana, you get used to rain. His cargo was another matter. Jake had, by most standards, plenty of money. After winding down Cane Oil & Gas, Jake had become a successful stockbroker and on the side had become a successful investor in several oil and gas prospects. Even if his wife ended up with half, he would still be well off and he had carefully kept all of the remaining Cane assets as his separate property. He did not need the money and he certainly did not require any additional aggravation. Yet, for no explainable reason, Jake continued west. One thought now occupied his mind, *what is in the cases?* Then it occurred to Jake, *what if there is a tracking device in one or both of those cases?* Could someone be tracking him?

In a few minutes, Jake came to Highway 222 with a sign pointing to I-40 and turned left. Minutes later he saw a truck stop that lit up the sky like the

Louisiana State Fair. He decided that he would rent a shower room and find out what he had.

Surprisingly, neither case was locked. The aluminum briefcase contained plastic bags filled with white powder. No surprise. Jake had avoided the drug scene and had little idea what was in those bags, but he knew that this powder was valuable. The rolling case was made from a lite nylon reinforced fabric. Jake opened it quickly before considering that it might be booby-trapped. It was not and it contained exactly what Jake had guessed, cash. Lots of cash. He was now cognizant of the possibility of a booby trap. Jake had read in the paper about a bank robber some years earlier had been given a wad of money that exploded in his face and covered him with ink. Jake gingerly removed each of the carefully bundled stacks of bills weighing each to see if any was heavier than any other. This decidedly unscientific endeavor revealed no perceptible differences among the bundles and thankfully no ink. Jake had handled all of the money and found nothing but money. Only then did he notice the pocket on the inside of the aluminum case.

Jake's attention turned back to the aluminum case and he carefully unzipped the pocket, empty. But in searching the pocket he felt a bulge in the lining. As he probed the lining, Jake felt a small square object thicker but smaller than a credit card. He ripped out the lining and carefully removed the object, a black square piece of molded plastic with what appeared to be Chinese writing. Was this piece of plastic a homing device? Jake did not immediately panic. After all, he had expected to find exactly what he had found and it had been less than an hour since he had left the former owners of this suitcase dead in a vacant lot. He was in a busy truck stop. Jake quickly locked his shower room and walked slowly and deliberately out the trucker's entrance to the truck stop to the pumps where the truckers were filling up their rigs. Jake's idea was to casually throw the homing device into the bed of an 18 wheeler and to send it off to parts unknown. Jake was well pleased with this idea until he realized that every truck he could see and, there were a many trucks, had box or van trailers and they were all closed, locked and sealed. Now panic set in, as did paranoia. Every trucker now looked like a gangbanger and the patrolling sheriff's deputy driving through the parking lot almost sent Jake over the edge. Just as he was about to vomit Jake passed by yet another box trailer only to see a Dodge Ram 3500 hot shot dually with a 20-foot goose neck trailer attached. Jake knew that the trailer was loaded with equipment destined for an oil well somewhere. As Jake approached he heard the truck fire up and saw the rig began to move. Jake hastily flipped the black square into the back of the dually just as it drove off. Jake looked around, the sheriff's deputy was parked and on his way to the café, he took no notice of Jake. No one had seen him dispose of the tracking device, or so Jake thought. No one, that is, except for the truck stop surveillance cameras.

The rain had stopped as he slowly drove away from the truck stop. It after 2:30 a.m. and Jake was dangerously tired. Even with the strong truck stop coffee, the windows wide open and the radio turned up way too loud, he could barely keep his eyes open. Joe Stampley and Moe Bandy were singing *"Roll on Big Mama"* as Jake drove west on I-40. Almost every other vehicle on the road was an 18 wheeler. Jake needed to find a place to sleep.

CHAPTER 4 - *HEY GOOD LOOKIN'.*
Hank Williams
https://www.youtube.com/watch?v=PsjTp77LBHA

Jake always had a girlfriend, usually one from a good Shreveport family with blond hair and teeth straightened by a high priced orthodontist. Some of his relationships involved some pretty serious teenage lust, but when the passion died down the relationships soon fizzled.

Jake was a KA at LSU as had been his father and grandfather before him. As a fraternity member Jake was expected to and did date sorority girls. There were plenty of them and plenty of parties mostly revolving around LSU football, which is akin to religion in Baton Rouge.

In those college days, Jake had no ambition and no plans nor even thoughts about the future. LSU was a great place to be, especially if your grandparents were supplying enough cash and Jake's were. Life was good with school and classes a mere annoyance, an annoyance Jake realized to be necessary if he intended to stay in Baton Rouge. So Jake went to class and "studied" history, a major Jake liked and, more importantly, a major that required the least amount of actual work.

It was in a vast Louisiana history class in the spring of Jake's junior year that he first saw Jeannette Richard (pronounced ReeCharde). Jeannette was walking out of the class that first time. She wore a tee shirt, tight jeans and jogging shoes. Her dress was not the appropriate dress of an LSU sorority sister. But what really caught Jake's attention as she walked in front of him was her behind. And not just the behind that one of his fraternity brothers would later describe as "world class" but the way that behind moved in those jeans. Each butt cheek had a little hiccup with every stride. Jake would never know if that movement was natural or learned. He was smitten, or was it lust again? He didn't care; Jake had to meet this girl.

LSU was and is a big school with thousands of students. The Greek community was not as big and a relatively good looking frat boy like Jake could easily arrange to meet any of the sorority girls on campus. Jake soon found out that Jeannette was not in a sorority and he really did not know how to meet a GDI (god damn independent). Jake had always associated with the same crowds, and he had always known everyone he needed to know. Worse yet, try as he might, during the weeks following that first sighting, Jeannette was showing no interest at all in Jake.

Jeannette was not the most beautiful girl on the LSU campus but the more she ignored Jake, the more enamored he became. While Jeannette might not be described as beautiful, she was magnetic and beautiful in her own way. She was tall, probably five foot eight and slim, but not skinny, more muscular than skinny. Jake would later learn that she was a runner. Her hair was dark brown, cut shorter than most. She had brown eyes, the naturally brown skin of a Cajun, and a lively, inviting face. She had a scar on her chin and an ever so slightly bent nose, relics Jake would later learn from her days as a high school hurdler. These imperfections somehow made Jeannette even more attractive. Men loved her and strangely the girls also liked her. Jeannette had plenty of girlfriends and plenty of suitors. She did not need and was not interested in some spoiled, immature, rich frat boy, especially one from

Shreveport. Yes, Jeannette had noticed Jake and yes, she was a bit curious about him.

The more Jeannette ignored Jake, the more determined he became to arrange a meeting. Jake had learned that Jeannette was from Chalmette, a suburb of New Orleans. Not many sorority girls ascend from Chalmette, Louisiana. But some do and one, in particular, turned out to be a cousin of Jeannette, a DZ, and a Golden Girl, to boot. Jake later realized that he was acting like some junior high bimbo, but at the time it all seemed necessary. Jake befriended Jeannette's cousin, who was interested in a rich frat boy, with the sole and only intention of securing an introduction to Jeannette. It's good when a scheme pans out, and on that fateful night at a bar in Tiger Land, Jake, on a date with Jeannette's cousin, was finally introduced to his dream girl. Unfortunately for Jake, Jeannette had secured her dream date on that same night. To Jake's dismay his introduction to Jeannette included an introduction to Jeannette's date, a hero to everyone in Baton Rouge, the LSU starting quarterback. While Jake was reasonably good looking and in reasonably good shape, he was ordinary and puny in the shadow of

Jeannette's date. As they stood at the bar drinking beer, it became increasingly clear that the quarterback was only interested in himself and to a lesser extent Jeannette's truly beautiful cousin and that Jake was only interested in Jeannette. Before the night was over the quarterback and the Golden Girl went off together and Jake was obliged to take Jeannette home in the 3 Series BMW his grandparents had bought him for high school graduation. Not about to push his luck, Jake did not even get out of the car at Jeannette's apartment but, he did drive off with her phone number.

As he headed back to the frat house, Jake switched to the local classic country station already programmed into his radio. Hank Williams was singing one of his classics, *Hey Good Lookin, to* which Jake sang along, off key.

CHAPTER 5 - *A FAMILY TRADITION.*
Hank Williams, Jr
https://www.youtube.com/watch?v=IHjaW9sXl7s

It was less than an hour from the truck stop on Highway 222 and I-40 to the Peabody Hotel. Jake had stayed at the Peabody before and decided on the basis of his newfound wealth and the fact that he could not keep his eyes open that he would check in and get some sleep. It was between 3:30 and 4:00 am, but the valet was awake and cheerful. Jake thought that only an exceptional hotel would have an attentive staff at this time of the morning. He handed the valet five dollars to watch his car while he checked with the desk to see if a room was available. The lobby of the Peabody is one of the grandest in the South. Memphites would argue that it tops the Fairmont Hotel, now the Roosevelt Hotel, in New Orleans. On this early morning the exquisite fountain was empty, no water and no ducks. The water had been drained and several florists were on ladders busily constructing a new floral arrangement at the top of the fountain. Through blood shot eyes, Jake admired the ornate ceiling, wondering how the stained glass stayed in place. What a strange thought. A stressed and sleep-deprived mind is easily distracted. Yes, they had a room, not cheap, and Jake took it and returned to his car for the luggage, two rolling bags, and one aluminum briefcase. Jake really did not want to lose sight of his bags, especially the newly acquired ones, but decided to allow the bell boy to take his luggage so as not to draw attention. Safely in his room, Jake fell immediately into a deep sleep and did not wake up until well after the ducks had made their journey from the roof to the lobby.

Jake woke up to a bright, beautiful August morning and after hanging the Do Not Disturb sign; he went downstairs for some coffee and a roll. The lobby was now alive with people, some already drinking the Bloody Mary's being prepared off to one side. Jake stepped outside. It was already getting hot, but he did not stay outside for long. For perhaps the first time in his life, Jake had decided that he needed a plan and that the plan needed to begin with an inventory of exactly what was in the bags up in his room.

There was not much that Jake could do with the packages of white powder. Once he got back to

Shreveport Jake knew someone who would know all about the contents of the aluminum briefcase and would probably know how to get rid of it. The money was another matter. Jake knew about money and knew how hard it had become to launder money. He was wondering if the drugs would be easier to dispose of than would be the money. Then he realized the drugs would likely be turned into money and would leave him with the same problem times two. Jake as not at all certain that his plan when formulated would include the sale of these drugs. He would have to think about that; two years ago there would have been no thinking. Jake would not have taken the briefcase in the first place and if he had he would have thrown the drugs into the Mississippi River.

The money was another matter. As a young man, Jake always thought that too much money was a problem he could easily solve. He had always loved money, he thought, no, he knew that if he had enough money Shreveport would forget about his father and embrace Jake as his own man. But, the money he was now about to count was a different kind of money. Early in Jake's career as a stockbroker, a potential client, the owner of a successful restaurant, came to him with a suitcase full of money similar to the case Jake was about to inventory. Even then he knew this was a problem. One cannot just deposit large sums of money into a brokerage account or into a bank account without catching the attention of the IRS, the FBI, and who knew what other law enforcement agencies. The crooked restaurateur had been summarily sent away to find some other home for his money. Using money that had not been first taxed was going to be a problem.

Jake took the money out of the briefcase, still being careful to check for booby traps. He found nothing but money, no ink, and no more tracking devices. There were three denominations of dollars: twenty's, fifty's and hundred's. There were only ten bundles of twenty's and they were bundled in purple straps. Each bundle contained four bundles of twenty dollar bills each or one hundred bills or $2,000. The twenty's totaled $20,000.

Not nearly enough to die for.

There were no visible marks on the twenty's and no discernable pattern to the serial numbers. Jake thought that if he were going to mark the money he would probably mark the larger bills. There were even fewer fifty's, they were bundled in brown straps, and each bundle contained five smaller bundles with twenty bills in each bundle. There were four bundles of fifty's equaling $20,000. No markings, no pattern.

Not worth dying for.

The rest were hundred dollar bills. The United States no longer prints bills larger than the one hundred dollar bill. And there were a lot of hundred's, all bundled in gold straps. Each bundle had ten smaller bundles of ten bills each, $100 X 10 X 10=$10,000. There were 126 bundles of one hundred dollar bills equaling $1,260,000, making the grand total exactly $1,300,000.

But…is even that enough to warrant killing and dying? Jake did not think so, but he had not killed anyone and had no intention of ever killing anyone.

By the time Jake had finished counting the money, it was afternoon and he was getting hungry. On a whim, Jake decided to call his fraternity brother, William Thomas Jefferson, or as he was known in college Billy Bone or just Boner. Boner was from a wealthy Memphis family who owned tugboats and barges that plied the Mississippi River from Joplin to New Orleans and into the Intercostal Canal. Boner worked at the family business but would have probably been unemployed if not for the fact that his father owned the business. Not that Boner was stupid, far from it; in fact, his fraternity brothers would all say that Boner was the most intelligent person they knew. But Boner had no need to work; he had all that any young man could want, lots of money and a big dick. You could say that Boner's dick was legendary and he was not at all shy about showing it even in mixed company. These sightings usually occurred after Boner had a few drinks, a not infrequent occurrence. In addition to his wealth, intelligence, and dick, Boner was also kind, affable, generous, humorous, athletic, and handsome. Boner had it all in college and probably still did somewhere inside, but he had never grown up. Recently divorced from his third wife, he was still the same Boner he had been in college. This was the exact reason Jake was calling him. Jake had grown up and being grown up had not turned out to be a fun and desirable accomplishment.

Billy, as he was known by most people in Memphis, answered immediately.

And as luck would have it, he had arrived late to work and had not had lunch. Jake was in Memphis and he wanted bar-b-que. Boner would know the best place and it would not likely be the famous Rendezvous. Memphites are connoisseurs of bar-b-que and they each have a favorite joint that each will argue is the best of all. In Boner's expert opinion, the best bar-b-que in Memphis can only be found at Central BBQ and only at the original Central BBQ on Central Ave. Boner's driver's license was under suspension due to a recent DUI, so Jake agreed to pick him up in front of his office not far from the Peabody.

The first thing Boner did was ask about Jake's ex-wife, Jen. Boner never tried to hide the fact of his undying love for Jeannette Richard. Some blamed Boner's failures in matters of the heart on this unrequited love for Jen. Boner among them. Yet, Boner remained a gentleman and while he came close to inappropriate advances, he never went too far. Now that Jake and Jen were separated Boner planned to wait the appropriate period of time and then he would clean up his act and go after Jen.

Jake knew this, Boner had told him so in no uncertain terms. Jake was not the least offended nor was he concerned about Boner's intensions. Jake knew full well that the worst enemy of his relationship with Jen was neither Boner nor the many others who yearned for Jen's attention.

The enemy was Jake.

"She rarely talks to me and then only when necessary."

"She's dating this guy named Joe, a wealthy playboy, probably screwing him."

"I don't know if it's revenge or if she is through with me forever."

Boner was intrigued by these three statements from Jake.

"I hope she is through with both of you. Once she gets some of this," pointing to his dick, "She'll forget about everyone else," he said. Jake wondered why he did not punch Boner. He wanted to, and if anyone other than Boner had said the same thing, Jake probably would have. But Boner was Boner, he just was.

"Yea, right, just like your first three wives," Jake said.

"Everybody makes mistakes, me more than some, but if I ever get a chance with Jen, I won't fuck up again." Boner added, "You, Jake, are a fool, period." Nothing else was said on the subject of Jen. They both knew that Jen would never love Boner, a fact Boner was not prepared to accept.

As, could often happen around Boner, the ribs and beers at the late lunch turned into late afternoon drinks at Boner's favorite bar and led to a drunken trip to what was then a Memphis institution, a "gentleman's club" called Platinum Plus.

As Jake entered the bar, he saw a nearly nude girl dancing awkwardly to some song he had never heard turned up entirely too loud. The scene caused Jake to think about his father. John Cane would have liked this place. Boner was obviously well known at

Platinum Plus. He and Jake were ushered to a table near, but not too close to the stage and were soon joined by the "terrific" Tricksy and her friend the "magnificent" Madison. Jake would soon learn (and later witness) that these girls were famous for their girl on girl act which they performed nightly, a show that looked natural for these two gifted entertainers, or so Jake thought in his increasingly inebriated state. Jake had some serious cash and as he got drunker and drunker, he thought that this was an excellent way to launder money. The girls agreed and were professionals at helping.

It was late when Boner, Jake, Tricksy, and Madison left the bar. The girls were smart enough to hail a cab. Jake left his car in the parking lot with the cars of a few other patrons too drunk to drive home. Boner wanted to go back to the Peabody but Jake, even intoxicated, was smart enough not to take these girls back to his room filled with drugs and cash, so they went to Boner's house near downtown. Jake didn't know where he was, but he felt safe with Boner in Boner's town at Boner's house. At the house, the girls were enticed to reprise a shortened version of their show and, needless to say, a good time was had by all, especially Boner. Not to say that Jake did not have fun but he was, after all still legally married and the fun was tempered by a fair amount of guilt that would linger. Jake was not a big drinker, but he had been drunk a few times, mostly at LSU, and when drunk he had done and said things that he later wished he had left unsaid and undone. Unlike some drunks, Jake did not forget these things when he sobered up. Jake was pre-disposed to carry such uncomfortable memories with him as unwanted baggage. He knew right from wrong. The whole night had been another bad decision.

When Jake made bad decisions, his mother would often remind him of the many bad decisions his father often made. Eloise would often say, "The fruit doesn't fall far from the tree." At times like these Jake sought to blame his father for his behavior, knowing full well that his mother would not have bought that excuse. "Be your own man, Jake. Take responsibility for your decisions," she would preach.

CHAPTER 6 - *YOUNG LOVE.*
Sonny James
https://www.youtube.com/watch?v=pU_8D5jBqd0

In the days following their introduction, Jake played it cool. He did not call Jeannette, but after their next history class, he caught up with Jeannette and was able to talk her into going to the student union for a cup of coffee.

The courtship progressed slowly from there and after a few cups of coffee after class Jeanette eventually agreed to go on an actual Friday night date consisting of a movie and a late meal at Poor Boy LLOYD'S downtown. The meeting went well, and to Jake's surprise, he discovered that there was more to this girl than the initial physical attraction.

More importantly, Jeannette was warming to Jake, who took on a different personality when he was alone with her. Jake was quieter when he was with Jeannette and not at all his usual cocky frat self. He liked Jeannette, was interested in what she said, and was uncharacteristically more respectful of Jeanette than he had ever been with any female, save his mother.

The relationship progressed with several dates but to Jake's chagrin little physical contact, nothing more than a goodnight kiss.

At LSU, the Kappa Alpha fraternity has the Old South Spring Formal every year and this year was no different. Fraternity brothers such as Jake were expected to ask sorority girls to such events, it was an unwritten rule. Jake had a dilemma. Should he take a sorority girl? The Golden Girl was back on the market. Should he pass on the formal altogether or should he break the rules and ask Jeannette. Looking back, none of this appears to be much of a problem but at the time it was a real dilemma. Jake thought seriously about giving up on Jeannette and taking the Golden Girl. He was pretty sure he could score with Jeannette's cousin who was, after all, truly gorgeous. Jake thought about the entrance he could make with Jeannette's beautiful cousin on his arm.

At this time in Jake's life, he more often than not made good decisions, even if there was no real long-term plan. Although probably not his best choice, Jake decided to do the obvious, he would talk to Jeannette about his dilemma and he did. The conversation took place over lunch at the Pastime Restaurant, more of a bar, referred to in Baton Rouge simply as the Pastime. It was a warm spring day and Jeannette wore a tee shirt with a built-in bra, showing a little cleavage, a pair of daisy dukes, and her usual running shoes.

She was stunning and the head of every man in the joint followed her as she moved about, when she entered, when they ordered, and when they found a table in the side room. These shorts were probably last year's model and Jeannette had filled out some since then. The bottom of her "world class" ass was almost visible as it characteristically moved in those blue jean cut-offs. Her runner's legs were long, brown and shapely, perfect. Jake should have made his decision right then but his lust temporarily clouded his thinking and he proceeded with the discussion.

Predictably Jeannette was fine with whatever Jake decided. She understood that she was a GDI and a Yat to boot. She also knew how out of place she would feel at a KA formal. Jake should probably take Goldie, Jeannette's cousin, or so Jeannette said.

While it is doubtful that any man can ever really understand a woman, Jake was no exception but he could make good decisions and he made one. By now he knew Jeannette and she was lying. If he was ever to have the relationship with Jeannette that he craved he had two choices stay home from the formal or take Jeannette, unwritten rules be damned. In fact, he had only one choice. Take Jeannette if she would still go.

At first Jeannette said no, she was not happy to have been one of the several choices. Jake persisted and when it became apparent that he would not go without her Jeannette relented and reluctantly agreed to go. Jeannette was genuinely attracted to Jake and, perhaps as importantly, her cousin's formal dress was available for Jeannette to wear.

Jake picked up Jeannette wearing the double breasted tuxedo his grandmother had bought him at Jordan & Booth. All men look better in a tux and Jake knew that he looked good. There was a strut in his walk that became more pronounced when Jeannette opened her apartment door. Jeannette wore a long white form fitting dress that accented her tan, her ass and revealed just the right amount of cleavage. In her high heels, Jeannette was almost as tall as Jake. She was in a word, striking, more feminine than she had been before.

When they walked into the formal, fashionably late, everyone noticed. Few of Jake's fraternity brothers had seen Jeannette before but they were all impressed. Not one of his brothers was concerned about the fact that she was not a Greek, nor were they concerned about where she was raised. Rather, each brother was intent on meeting this vision and each of their dates was immediately jealous. Jake relished in the attention, but Jeannette was uncomfortable and self-conscious. A glass of jungle juice was a necessity.

Within a year most of the girls would come to like Jeannette and some of them would even become lifelong friends. But on that first night the chorus from the mouths of those present was "who is this bitch?" In this setting, Jeannette was never totally comfortable and even though Jake stayed close by, she understandably drank a little too much. Jake had to steady Jeannette when they left the party. Of course, by then almost everyone had too much to drink and no one seemed to notice.

In the early morning hours after the formal, Jake finally saw Jeannette naked for the first time. In the dim light of her bedroom, he could now see that he had been wrong, Jeannette was definitely the most beautiful girl on the campus of LSU and probably in all of Louisiana.

She had tan lines of a runner, not bikini lines but the lines where she had been covered by a jog bra and running shorts. Her breasts were smallish but not too small. Her bush was dark almost black and thick with unusually soft hair. Jake had never desired a girl more than he did at that moment. The first time did not last long at all, but Jake remained hard and the second time he lasted long enough for Jeannette to finish, more than once. Jeannette told him that she had never come like that before. He wanted to believe her and he did, without question.

When they awoke in the morning, Jake was certain that his feelings were beyond lust. Jake was in love, for the first and last time. They stayed together that whole Sunday, mostly in bed and for a long time were rarely far from each other. When, after months of being almost exclusively together, they began to interact with others. Their friends would talk of them as the perfect couple, obviously in love.

This was the beginning of great times for Jake and Jen as he now called her. When Sonny James sang "*Young Love,*" Jake thought of Jen and sometimes shivered when he remembered how close he had been to losing her at the Pastime that spring afternoon. As if the restaurant was responsible for his immaturity, from that day on, Jake never again darkened the door of the Pastime.

CHAPTER 7- *AM I THAT EASY TO FORGET?* Jim Reeves
https://www.youtube.com/watch?v=GTmMDhvhXZc

Jake awoke to the smell of coffee. Boner was up and dressed when Jake stumbled from the guest room. Jake had a cotton mouth, a queasy stomach, and a pounding headache. Boner was no worse for the wear. People who drink as much as Boner, rarely get hangovers. Boner called it being *in drinking shape*.

Boner said to Jake, "You look liked hammered shit. You got to practice if you want to hang with 'the Boner'." What had seemed like a good idea yesterday, hanging with "the Boner", did not seem like a good idea now. Jake was not interested in getting in shape to hang *with "the Boner."*

The local news was on and the lead story being reported was about four men who had been found shot to death on the outskirts of a nearby town. The newscaster went on to inform the public that another man had been severely wounded and was under police protection at an undisclosed hospital.

Two of the dead were undercover narcotics officers the other three were employees of a local construction company with no known criminal records. No drugs or contraband of any sort had been found at the site, just guns and spent casings. The group had actually been discovered yesterday morning, but officials had delayed the release of information while they notified next of kin and gained a head start on the investigation.

Jake said nothing.

Boner, on the other hand, was full of comments. It seemed that Boner knew the owner of the construction company; a man named Robert Daniel Stephens III aka Dan or more often called simply Big D. Big D lived around the corner from Boner in one of those houses on the bluff overlooking the river. The construction company owned by Big D was D-Line Construction, a large corporation with jobs not only in Memphis but also in Nashville, Jackson, Little Rock, and even in Baton Rouge.

"How do you know so much about this Big D?" Jake wondered aloud.

Boner was happy to answer. "Because Big D also owns one of your favorite bars, Platinum Plus. Not just everyone knows that." Boner was animated. "And another thing, Big D and some of his high school buddies meet for breakfast at the Arcade on the fourth Wednesday (it was Wednesday, August 24, 2005) of every month and that's today." He paused. "Get dressed and let's go down there, see if he shows up."

The statement was more of a command than a suggestion, so Jake showered and put on the same clothes he had worn the day before. While dressing, Jake discovered that his wallet was intact and all of his credit cards were there. He was somewhat surprised about that bit of good fortune; however he was not surprised that all of the cash that had been in the wallet was gone. Jake was thankful for the fact that he had only lost his cash. He still had plenty of money back in his room.

As the coffee helped lift the fog from his brain, he remembered something else, "Boner, I don't have any money and we don't have a car," He told his longtime friend when he stepped back into the living room.

"Not to worry. We can walk to the Arcade they take credit cards and I have a stash of cash." Boner made no mention of his job which made Jake realize that he had told his office that he would be back today.

"No problem," Boner retorted, "Use my computer to email them that you have been delayed, the world will not come to an end if the star stock bookie of Shreveport misses a few days of work."

Jake wanted to get his car and the bounty and to get the hell out of Memphis, but he also had more than a passing interest in the man who employed two of the dead men and the one live man Jake had left for dead yesterday morning. Surely, Big D would not show for his monthly meeting, but Boner would not take no for an answer.

The ribs Jake ate yesterday were the only food Jake had consumed in over twenty-four hours. Jake's queasy stomach needed food. It was a short walk to the Arcade. Boner assured him that they would find a cab at the Arcade to take them to get Jake's car.

The Arcade is one of the oldest restaurants in Memphis. Elvis frequented the Arcade in his early days and is said to have sat at a table in the back left corner. The Elvis' table. Big D's group always sat at The Elvis' table and as was often the case was forced to wait outside until the table could be cleaned and set for the group. Big D's group consisted of about six regulars and occasionally as many as ten. The common thread for these men was a high school football team in a small Arkansas town about forty miles from Memphis. These men had been the core of that team. A team that garnered the only state championship that town ever won. These men were the seniors from that team and from such a small town they had all known each other forever. Another thing kept this group together, success. All ten of these men were successful to one degree or another. There were several businessmen like Big D, a corporate lawyer, two college professors, an insurance broker, an accountant, a stockbroker and Ronald Terrence Kelley aka Kelley, the head of drug enforcement for District 4 of the Tennessee Highway Patrol.

It was just a few blocks from Boner's house to the Arcade. As is often the case a crowd of tourists as well as locals had gathered on the sidewalk outside of the restaurant waiting for a table. Boner saw Big D and they passed pleasantries, they were not real friends and Big D made no pretense that they were. Big D was indeed a big man, probably six four and well over three hundred pounds. He had a large stomach, but he was solid, not fat. Maybe because of his size he appeared to be a bit disheveled. He wore designer jeans, at that size, probably made for him, an expensive blue blazer, a starched Western style white shirt, and black alligator boots. He had a big head with light brown, curly and somewhat unruly hair. Everything about him was big and intimidating, down to his flat nose and even his ears. D was not short for Dan, no, everyone in this group knew that D was short for defense because he had been such a dominating defensive tackle in high school that the coach began calling him "the defense" which was eventually shortened to "D" and at some point Big D for obvious reasons.

D, as he was more often called then, was more than simply the best high school tackle to ever play in his part of Arkansas, he was also the son of the richest man in town. His father owned timber land and the only bank in town. D's father was the well-respected and powerful president of the bank, a position from which he could smooth over the inappropriate, mean and sometimes even criminal activities of his son. Most people in the little town would have overlooked D's behavior because of his skills on the football field. All the others his father either bribed or intimidated. D was loved by many and secretly hated by many more. His mother was a true Arkansas beauty queen, a runner-up in the Miss Arkansas pageant. She married D's father for the money and prestige, but soon developed a hatred for the little town and her fat condescending husband. D's mother gradually filled her days with vodka and ice, rapidly deteriorated and died young.

As Jake was examining Big D, a smaller yet more intimidating man joined the group. Kelley was wearing a highway patrol uniform that fit him like a glove. He had blue bloodshot eyes that looked right through Jake and Boner. There was not an ounce of fat anywhere on Kelley's body. Kelley was probably Jake's height, but his arms were much larger than Jake's and it was easy to see the outline of his muscles through the uniform. Kelley had a light complexion and closely cropped blond hair, not one hair was out of place. While D's face was round and inviting, Kelley's face was sharp and thin. Kelley had been the quarterback on the team and the Captain. Kelley was the opposite of D. Kelley was a good student, a good citizen and the boy every man would have as his child. Kelley's father was the police chief in the town also respected especially by the upstanding members of the community. To the rest, the poor blacks in particular, Kelley's father was more feared than respected. He could be violent with anyone who violated his law. Kelley felt his father's temper at an early age and whenever he stepped out of the lines drawn by his father. It was far easier for Kelley to be a perfect son than it was to incur his father's wrath. Kelley secretly hated D, and would never understand why his father overlooked D's behavior. He overlooked behavior that would have resulted in a severe beating for Kelley. Kelley's mother was also a beauty, a local girl with apparently little else. She was subservient with seemingly no ambition. She never drank a single drop of alcohol and neither did Kelley. Police Chief Kelley would not allow alcohol or anyone who drank alcohol in his house. If he could have, he would have prohibited alcohol in his town. Kelley grew up in a house that was always in order, a house where dinner was on the table whenever his father came home from work.

The piercing eyes again caught Jake's attention as Kelley approached Big D and began to speak.

"What the hell were your people and your Escalade doing in Brownsville yesterday morning?" were Kelley's opening words.

"I was hoping you would tell me," replied Big D with no sign of any particular concern. "If your people would let me see Jessie I bet I could find out."

"Jessie is shot up and lawyered up, he is not talking to anyone," Kelley told him.

D turned the conversation. "The news reporter says that your people were there, some kind of sting operation gone bad?"

Kelley did not respond. The waiter was ready to seat Big D, Kelley and the others and they all moved inside and sat at their normal table. Boner and Jake were seated up front too far to monitor the conversation in the back corner. Boner ordered "Eggs Redneck" and Jake ordered the country fried steak breakfast, in a way a protest against Jen, who would never knowingly allow Jake to eat such unhealthy food. In his weakened condition, Jake had to literally fight back the tears as he thought about Jen.

Boner was right. Jake was a fool, period.

Jake had gone outside earlier to call Jen. Joe should have been at work, but it was obvious that Jen was not alone. Jake wanted to say "I love you". He wanted to tell her to get away from that son-of-a-bitch but he didn't, he couldn't get the words out. Jen was legally his wife but she was her own person and he had never told her what she could or could not do. She had never let him tell her what to do and she sure wasn't going to listen to him now. Jake made small talk about their children, John and Ellie then hung up. He returned to the restaurant with a huge lump in his chest. *Am I that easy to forget?*

CHAPTER 8 - *WOLVERTON MOUNTAIN.*
Claude King
https://www.youtube.com/watch?v=Izp1mjz__Xc

Summer came too fast for Jake and Jen. Jake was supposed to go home for the summer and work on a pipeline for one of his father's friends and Jen had a summer job selling women's clothing at D.H. Holmes on Canal Street in New Orleans. Neither of them wanted to leave the other, it is a long way from Shreveport to New Orleans, a good six-hour drive in those days.

As far as Jake knew, money was no problem. He seemed to have an unlimited budget, mostly from the Chandler side. Not so much for Jen. She had a small scholarship and some student loans. Her family barely had enough to take care of themselves and her younger brother and sister. They paid for part of Jen's apartment and sent Jen extra money when they could. Jen worked part time at a store selling running shoes to get by.

Jake was not good at planning, he didn't need to plan, he had mailbox money.

By now Jen had fallen as hard for Jake as he had for her. She did not want to go home for the summer and she did not want to lose Jake to some blond airhead in Shreveport. Jake was going to move out of the Frat house in the fall anyway. It would be easier and cheaper for Jake to get an apartment now than in the fall. Her plan: tell her parents that she needed a class only available in the summer, not exactly a lie; move into Jake's new apartment; and, work more hours at the shoe store.

Jake liked the idea and to graduate on time, he did actually need makeup classes for some he had dropped. Before he met Jen, Jake was aware of this problem but had decided that an extra fall football semester at LSU would be just fine. Jake could truthfully tell his family a similar story.

So it was that Jake and Jen moved in together in the summer between their junior and senior year, but, somehow the fact of their cohabitation was never clearly conveyed to either family.

Neither had ever lived with a person of the opposite sex.

At first it was a problem, Jake was used to having people pick up after him and Jen was not used to picking up after anyone and was not going to get used to it. This led to a few fights which led to passionate make-up sex. Jake almost looked forward to a fight, but he instinctively knew better than to manipulate her and it was seldom necessary. Jen claimed to have little sexual experience which was what Jake wanted to hear, no experience would have been even better news. Jen's sexual experience was growing as was Jake's. Jen was a willing and open lover, her initial inhibitions soon faded away and they became increasingly comfortable with each other. Life was good for Jake and Jen in that hot Baton Rouge summer.

By fall, the families had become aware of their children's sleeping arrangements but neither family had met their child's roommate (that is how Eloise referred to Jen). Jake and Jen were both afraid to introduce each other to their parents for some of the same reasons. Jen was afraid of what her dad might say or do and, Jake was afraid of the same type of thing from his mostly drunk father. He was also secretly afraid of what his mother might think of Jen. Jen had the accent of a Yat and she could never use the words take and bring correctly.

Eloise was a Southern lady and a bit of a snob. Which side would win out with Jen? If the snob side won out, he was going to side with Jen. Of that fact, he had no doubt.

Jake should not have worried. Late in the fall his mother and father came to Baton Rouge for a football game and took the roommates out to dinner at Ruth's Chris Steak House. Before the night was over Jen had won them over by being herself. Jen's parents would not be so easy.

Jen's father, Paul Richard, quit school in the eighth grade and went to work. He did various jobs each one better than the last. He learned how to read and educated himself by reading a variety of books and the *Times-Picayune* religiously and was able to get a G.E.D. Eventually, through his father who was a precinct leader in the Irish Channel, Paul got on as a stevedore loading and unloading ships on the docks.

He made good money for a laborer. He was short, a little taller than his favorite daughter and thick. He had the dark skin that his daughter inherited. Paul married Jen's mother, Hanna Constance, when they were both young; he was 17 and she was 16. Jeannette was born less than nine months later and Jen's sister and brother followed within four years. Hanna was tall, light skinned, Irish and Catholic. Hanna stayed home with the children but was now thinking about going to work since her last child was about to graduate from high school.

Jen put off introducing Jake to her parents as long as she could but when her great uncle died she had to go home and her mother made it abundantly clear that she better bring Jake. The wake was on a Friday. Jake and Jen drove to Chalmette after Jen got off of work. When they arrived, the wake was almost over and Jen's father had been drinking for hours. Jen was her father's favorite child and he did little to hide that fact. She was the oldest. She was independent, yet loving and had never caused any trouble.

Jen introduced Jake to her father. He was sitting at a table with Jen's mother. He might have said "Hello I'm glad to meet you," but he did not. Instead the first words from Paul Richard were, "So you are the little son of a bitch who has been laying the pipe to my beautiful daughter?"

Paul's accent was thick but Jake had been in South Louisiana long enough that he was pretty sure he understood Paul correctly and Jen later confirmed that he had. Jake had been rehearsing with Jen's help the conversation he would have with Jen's father, but Jake was not prepared for this and neither was Jen. No one spoke for a few seconds as Jake studied Paul wondering if he should run or die in place. But as Jake looked at Paul he could see that there was no malice in his eyes only reluctant acceptance that his baby was growing up and there was nothing he could do about it.

At last Jake responded. "Hello, Mr. Richard. I am Jake Cane, and I love your beautiful daughter." So began a loving relationship between Jake Cane and Paul Richard that was to last for 20 years. Jake had climbed *Wolverton Mountain* and Paul was no Clifton Clowers. Jen's mother was another matter. Jen's mother never warmed to Jen's rich Protestant, frat boy and now openly detested him.

CHAPTER 9 - *THE RIDE.*
David Allan Coe
https://www.youtube.com/watch?v=S6uR1rZjKkM

Jake and Boner took a cab to Platinum Plus and picked up Jake's car. After he dropped Boner at his office, he returned to the Peabody, gathered his luggage, and then started home. He popped his David Allan Coe CD into the player.

On the best of days, Jen would only just tolerate country music. The only good thing about their separation was that he could now choose the music he played in the car. "*The Ride,*" now that's old school. Good music to start a long road trip.

Kelley had been up for most of the previous twenty-four hours when Jake had seen him at the Arcade. It took hours for him to surreptitiously remove the tracking device from the Black Chevy Tahoe and by the time he began tracking it, the chip was out of range. Overnight he had driven from Nashville to Little Rock, no luck. After, breakfast he would be heading toward Jackson, he did not know what else to do. Yes, two undercover officers were dead in the drug deal that had gone wrong, but no, it was not an official operation of the Tennessee Highway Patrol. In fact, the only people in the Highway Patrol who knew anything about the operation were Kelley and Kelley's cohorts who were now dead. The living participant, Jessie, might be able to help, but there was no way for Kelley to get to Jessie. Jessie was being guarded by the DEA and FBI in addition to higher ups from Highway Patrol headquarters. It was only a matter of time until he would be facing some tough questions. Thankfully the only people who could tie Kelley to the drug deal were themselves dead. Kelley would survive. He always did.

News of the deaths had not come as quickly to Big D but when it did he was also worried that he might be implicated. Big D was a successful drug dealer and only a mediocre contractor. Competitors of D-Line Construction questioned how D-Line could make money the way they bid jobs and the answer was, they could not. D-Line Construction was a front for Big D's drug business. The construction business existed primarily for the purpose of laundering drug money and the cash money skimmed from Platinum Plus.

Big D and some silent partners were out 1.3 million dollars. They wanted their money back.

Big D's best men had been sent to the drug buy and they were now dead or in custody. The dead ones did not worry him as much as did the one who was still alive, Jessie.

Jessie was well aware of the fact that men who crossed Big D usually ended up as part of a foundation of a building or at the bottom of the Mississippi River. Jessie was not the strongest of Big D's henchmen and Big D was rightfully worried. Big D still had people. He first dispatched money to Jessie's family to get him a lawyer and the lawyer to get was specified. As Jake drove west on I-40 approaching Little Rock, Big D was anxiously awaiting a call from the specified lawyer. Jessie was a serious and dangerous problem.

When he got word that a man had grabbed the drugs and money and had left in a white Ford Police Interceptor, he was not surprised. He immediately concluded that dirty cops took the money, the drugs, killed four men and would blame the killings on "vicious drug dealers."

Big D wanted his money back. And he was thinking that Kelley might unknowingly help him find the dirty cops when he got the call from Pinky.

Pinky was the head bouncer at Platinum Plus. How Pinky got his name was a mystery and Big D did not really care. What Big D liked about Pinky was that he was loyal and a psychopath. Pinky would do anything Big D asked him to do with no conscious. As soon as he was paid Pinky conveniently forgot everything about the assignment. Pinky had killed men for Big D and if Big D asked about the killing a month later, Pinky would deny any knowledge. Pinky was a scary individual, over six feet tall and naturally muscled. He was dark, probably part black and he could stop most trouble at the club with a look. Pinky rarely called Big D and even though Big D's mind was on things other than the Club, he took the call.

"Boss, I thought you might want to know, someone left a White Ford Police Interceptor at the club last night. I think some dumb undercover cop is spying on us. Do you want me to see if I can find out who left that car?"

As Kelley drove south toward Jackson, Mississippi, he got a faint beep on the tracking device. The signal seemed to be coming from the west so he veered right onto I-20 and headed toward Monroe, Louisiana. As he headed west, the signal became increasingly stronger. Kelley checked the shells in his shotgun as he drove.

"I'm going to get you, you son of a bitch," he said out loud. As soon as he had the money and drugs, all witnesses would be eliminated. Kelley had no problem with killing anyone who crossed him. He could get away with murder because he saw to it that he or one of his cohorts investigated his murders. This time he may be out of state, but he would cover the murders or make it look like another drug deal gone bad. With his partners dead all of the money and drugs would be his. Kelley had over 20 years on the force. This might just be his last score. At 45, he was not as quick as he had once been and he was eligible for retirement. If he could save this deal, it might just be his ticket out.

CHAPTER 10 - *I LOVE YOU A THOUSAND WAYS*. Lefty Frizzell
https://www.youtube.com/watch?v=MJoWuVCYF0s

Jen was a good student. She was studying accounting and was near the top of her class. She was good with numbers and never had the luxury of getting a degree that would not lead to a good paying job. Fortunately for Jake, her study habits rubbed off on him and during his last year he took a few accounting classes and even an economic class as an elective. He had lots of time and he started cleaning up and cooking when Jen worked late at the store.

To be with Jen, he even took up jogging although he was never able to beat Jen in an actual 5K race.

They now visited their parents often. Eloise became increasingly enamored with Jen and Paul became increasingly tolerant of Jake. The couple was sickeningly (some of their friends would say) happy. Summer was approaching again as was graduation. Jen planned to get her CPA certification. Jake had no plans, maybe work for his dad? Could the family business support a new employee with no training or experience? For now Jake would have fun. His dad had told him "Don't get in a hurry to start working, once you start it never ends." Jake would later wonder if his dad would have given the same advice if he had been paying Jake's bills. Probably so, he concluded.

It was Saturday, May 7, 1983, and Jake, Jen, and some friends had made the semiannual trek to the Jazz Fest in New Orleans. It was hot, the beer was flowing and John Fred and the Playboys were on the main stage. Old people were dancing, singing, and drinking. Occasionally, one could catch a faint whiff of marijuana or as Paul Richard called it bambalacha. Tomorrow would be Mother's Day and Jake and Jen would spend part of the day with Jen's mother. One thing in particular was bothering Jen, she was late. Jen was also bothered by the fact that Jake was not in the least concerned.

After the Radiators had closed the Jazz Fest at 7:00 pm. the group went to the Quarter for more partying. In those days, no one had a cell phone so Jake did not get word of his father's death until he arrived at Jen's parents' house at almost midnight.

By then his father had been dead for over twenty-four hours. He was devastated and it took a lot of convincing to keep him from driving home that night.

It would be days before Jake learned the embarrassing details of his father's death and, then, only after his grandfather Chandler took him aside and told him.

Jake slept little and left early.

Jen stayed with her parents who were planning to drive up for the funeral. When the curse, as it was called in those days, did not, come Jen was inconsolable. If there was no problem surely the emotion would have caused her to start and there was another thing, she was nauseated every morning.

Jake was gone and, she thought, *what could he do anyhow*? He had the emotional maturity of a sixteen-year-old adolescent boy. At a time like that Jen did what most girls do, she told her mom.

It was Monday when Jen talked to her mother and before the day was over Jen had been to her doctor and it was confirmed, she was pregnant. Now, what? Her immature boyfriend was three-hundred miles away planning his father's funeral and she was pregnant with his child? Jen's entire family was Roman Catholic.

Abortion was out of the question. Adoption?

Marriage was a distant option for Jen and she suspected an untenable option for Jake. Jen was surprised by the support she got from her mother and when her father found out that night she was shocked by his support. Whatever happened, Jen would not go through this alone.

Meanwhile, Jake was in Shreveport planning his father's funeral and deeply missing Jen. The funeral would be held on Thursday morning at the big Methodist church at the head of Texas Avenue. It remained to be seen if the Richards would be in attendance. Somehow listening to his dad's old albums eased Jake's pain. When he talked to Jen on Tuesday night, she could hear Lefty Frizzell in the background. And when he said goodbye, Lefty was singing *I Love*

You a Thousand Ways, a song which summed up Jake's feelings for Jen far better than Jake could. No mention of Jen's *problem* was made.

Jake sensed something was wrong. He later convinced himself, if he had he not been so emotionally tied up with his dad's death, he would have at least asked Jen what was wrong?

CHAPTER 11- *HE STOPPED LOVING HER TODAY.* George Jones
https://www.youtube.com/watch?v=VExw77xJsBQ

It took Pinky about an hour to find out that Billy, *not everyone called him Boner*, had been with the man in the White Ford. Pinky had never thought to look at the license plate; if he had, he might have realized that a Tennessee cop would not be in a car with Louisiana plates. No one ever said that Pinky was the sharpest tack in the pack.

Big D wanted to question Billy, but he did not want to be implicated. If Pinky got involved, the connection to D was all too obvious. Big D went to the club to talk to Pinky in person, nothing would be said on a phone line and D would make a sign if possible. As an additional precaution, the music was turned up loud as D spoke to Pinky.

"I want to find out who owns that car, but I don't want you or anyone I know involved. Do you know someone who can find out what Billy knows?" He said.

"Sure, Boss. Prince Mario is out of jail and needs some money…he will find out. Plus, he knows how to keep his mouth shut."

D did not know Mario, which was good. "Just make sure that my name is never mentioned," Big D cautioned. "And another thing…find out from Tricksy if this yahoo was carrying a lot of cash."

"Oh yeah, he was," Pinky quickly piped up, feeling proud that he had answers for the boss. "Tricksy told me that there was no way the guy was a cop, too much money, and way too much class."

Mario Prince was an old friend Pinky knew mostly from prison. Mario, or as he called himself, Prince Mario, was out of jail awaiting trial for manslaughter and working as a painter. Mario only got bail because the DA could not produce any witness willing to testify.

Mario was quite willing to earn an extra hundred bucks. He could get the information Pinky needed—and he'd keep his mouth shut about it.

On the surface, Prince Mario was the nicest man you would ever want to meet. In the past, he had been a successful car salesman but he could not stay with anything. He liked to gamble and he was a pervert addicted to rough sex.

No one knew it, but he had drugged, raped and murdered the wife of a car dealer in Atlanta just because she had acted uppity toward him. Mario had enjoyed the activity so much that he had raped and murdered another rich woman in Nashville, a woman he did not even know.

Because Mario could not hold a job, he was always in debt. He stole things, mostly cars to pay off his debts. His stealing put him in jail where he learned how to survive. Mario was handsome, average size with dark hair and olive skin. As soon as he arrived in prison he was singled out to be the bitch for the leader of a prison gang. Mario had two choices, neither of which was good, kill or be sodomized.

As luck would have it, Pinky was the enforcer for a rival gang. Pinky knew Mario from clubs where he had worked in the past. He offered Mario an out, kill the leader of the rival gang and we will protect you. Pinky gave Mario a shiv.

When the gang leader came to rape Mario instead of a new young bitch, the gang leader got the shiv up under his rib cage and into his heart. The dead man was fifty pounds heavier than Mario and a convicted killer.

The prison guards knew what happened, but simply turned their heads. Everybody including the guards liked Mario and they were glad to be rid of the dead gang leader who had been disruptive and downright scary.

He would not be missed and no charges were ever filed.

Thus Mario became the member of Pinky's prison gang, feared and respected. Prince Mario was safe and would serve his time and, like Pinky, make parole.

It did take a while for Mario to find Billy and when he did, he couldn't believe the car in question belonged to a stock broker from Louisiana. Billy, or

Boner, was in his favorite bar drinking after work. As usual he had left work early.

The bar was almost empty and when the young barmaid went to the back for ice, Mario decided he would take the opportunity of privacy, and use it to beat the truth out of Billy. He also grossly underestimated the outwardly soft looking Billy.

Billy was indeed soft and a little over weight but he still worked out and he was nowhere near as soft as he appeared. And furthermore, Billy was an exceptional athlete, even if he was slightly over the hill.

Mario grabbed Billy by the neck and quickly learned a painful lesson. Billy was unprepared but never the less slapped Mario's hand away and came off the bar stool with a left-handed uppercut. He caught Mario under his chin and sent Mario reeling to the floor.

He was nearly unconscious as Billy grabbed him, kicked him, and threw him out of the front of the bar and onto Main Street where Pinky was waiting.

Needless to say, Pinky was not pleased with Mario's performance. There was no going back into the bar now, people who actually worked were getting off and the bar was filling with regulars; regulars who knew Billy.

"What happened?" Pinky barked at him. Mario explained everything to him, down to the moment that he learned too late that Billy, *Boner,* was left handed.

"Did you get the stock broker's name?" Pinky asked.

No, Mario didn't. And, he had caused a scene.

D would not be happy.

Pinky was not going back to D with no more information than he had now.

Pinky resolved to wait for Billy. He would help Mario to get the truth out of Billy once the regulars at the bar had their drinks and headed home.

Billy left the bar early, early for him. It was turning dark and he didn't have a car, so he decided to ride the street car down past the National Civil Rights Museum and then walk the rest of the way home.

As Pinky and Mario watched Billy board the street car, they slipped into their car and headed in the direction of Billy's house.

Tricksy had told Pinky where he lived and they would arrive long before Billy.

As Billy approached the front door to his house, he felt Mario behind him a split second before he felt a knife at his throat. "Open the door and keep quiet." Mario demanded.

Billy was now drunk, in no condition to resist. "What do you want?" Billy asked. "You can have my money, just take it. Let me go."

"Open the door." Billy recognized the voice from the bar. As Billy opened the door he was immediately shoved face first to the floor. "Now, tell me who owned the police car you were in at the club last night?"

"I told you, a stock broker friend from Shreveport, why is this so important?" Mario now thought that Billy was telling the truth.

"What's his name?" Mario asked.

"James Cane… he works for a big firm in Shreveport. Now will you leave me alone?"

Those were Billy's last words.

Mario rolled Billy over on his back and plunged the knife deep into Jake's friend's chest.

After Mario got up, he rolled Billy back over onto his stomach and removed Billy's wallet and gold watch.

Then he kicked Billy's dead body and walked out of the front door.

At first, Pinky was worried about Big D, but as it turned out, D was happy that there were no witnesses.

Later, when Jake learned of Billy's death, all he could think about was Billy's love for Jen.

Billy had, *Stopped Loving Her Today*.

It would not be long until Jake realized that he was likely the cause of his friend's death.

CHAPTER 12 – *ROUGHNECK.*
Johnny Cash
https://www.youtube.com/watch?v=2_H4w1Id7yE

The signal on the tracker continued to get stronger as Kelley passed Monroe and continued west on I-20. His receiver was now indicating that the disk was off to the south and he was about to make his first visit to an oil rig.

He would also learn the hard way that men who work on oil rigs are not easily intimidated.

Kelley came to Highway 34, the Jonesboro Road exit and turned south. From there he followed the road to La 548 and turned west.

Kelley was in the middle of nowhere.

The signal continued to get stronger until he passed a dirt road off to the south. It was now past dark. The dirt road led off into the woods, but the signal was coming from that direction so Kelley set off down the dirt road through the woods. The road was rough, but surprisingly wide.

Someone had been using this road—not just pickup trucks, large trucks had been down this road.

About a half mile off La 348, Kelley came to a clearing lit up with portable flood lights. In the clearing were numerous vehicles, including a Dodge Ram 3500 hot shot dually with a twenty-foot goose neck trailer attached.

The tracker was flashing and Kelley was stumped, *what the hell is going on here?*

Kelley had found the tracking disk.

It was somewhere in this well site.

The well site contained a full-size drilling rig. Some piece of equipment was stuck down in the drill bore and specialized hands were on site to fish the equipment out of the well. The frenzied activity revolved around that task. The owners of the well were paying a day rate for the drilling rig and the crew. Until the piece of equipment was removed, there could be no progress on the well. The operating company was watching its profits fade away. They had been trying to fish the stuck piece of equipment for twelve plus hours.

No one on the drill site was in the mood to visit with Kelley.

When he first got out of his Tennessee Highway Patrol Tahoe SUV, still in his uniform, a few of the roughnecks scurried off into the woods. It is not uncommon for a roughneck to have a warrant out for his arrest. The noise of diesel engines and the clamoring of the rig were deafening. Soon the crew noticed that Kelley was wearing a Tennessee patrolman uniform and was driving a Tennessee Patrol Unit. The fleeing roughnecks emerged from the woods and went back to work.

Even a roughneck knows that a Tennessee police officer has no authority in Louisiana. Kelley was out of his element. He figured that this was some kind of oil well, but exactly what they were doing and how the crew communicated in this noise was a mystery to him.

No one was the least bit interested in talking to Kelley, they simply ignored him and continued with their tasks. The only idle man was the driver of the hot shot truck, a man well known in the oil field, Harold Hixson.

Harold was about sixty years old and he'd been working in the oil fields for over forty-five years. Like many he had started as a roughneck and eventually worked his way up to driller. By the time Harold and Kelley met, Harold had worked at just about every position there was in the oil field. At some point Harold had gotten hurt, had taken a settlement, and bought the truck Kelley was examining. Harold now operated a hot shot service.

In the day and a half since Jake had thrown the tracking disk into the back of the truck, Harold had driven over a thousand miles.

Harold was about five-foot eight and weighed about two hundred and fifty pounds. Kelley was strong from working with weights and was trained in every manner of criminal restraint. Harold was stronger from forty-five years of hard work and as a younger man had been a notorious bar room brawler. In the oil field, no one messed with Harold, for good reason.

Kelley approached Harold and asked him his name.

"Harold" was the man's reply.

Kelley asked him, "Is this your truck?

"Maybe," Harold replied.

Kelley next asked, "What's going on here?" as he looked out over the rig.

"It's a circus!" Harold replied. "Follow me… I'm going to take a shit and if I shit a cougar you can shoot it with your gun."

The oil field humor was obviously lost on Kelley.

"Can I look in your truck?" Kelly asked. The receiver was indicating that the disk was in the truck.

"No, but you can look up my ass while I shit so you can get a head start on the cougar." More oil field humor. That was enough.

Kelley was no more than five feet from Harold but before he could draw his gun, he found himself flat on his face with a two hundred fifty pound man sitting on his back.

He couldn't see much from his position, but he could see a few roughnecks clapping, laughing and hollering. The crew had liked the show. Harold knew they would.

"It's time for you to answer some questions." The stocky man said to Kelley, "What is the Tennessee Highway Patrol doing in the middle of the Louisiana woods?"

Kelley was not used to answering anyone's questions and he was thinking if there had been any way for him to get up; it would be this redneck's ass. But there was no way and when Kelley reached for his revolver, Harold grabbed the gun and threw it half way into the woods. Then he did the same with Kelley's mace.

Sometimes, a straight answer is the best option.

Kelley was pretty sure that the man sitting on his back was not the man who had killed his men and stolen his money. If this man had 1.3 million dollars, he would be in some roadhouse buying drinks for every woman in the place.

A man with 1.3 million dollars would not be working at an oil well in the middle of the night.

"We set up a sting operation; we were trying to catch a big-time drug dealer. The operation went bad, two of my men were killed and someone got away with the drugs and money. We planted a tracking chip with the drugs and I think it is in your truck." Kelley told Harold.

Harold had seen many a fine hand ruined by drugs and he had no patience with anyone in the drug business. Harold immediately got off of Kelley, helped him up and shook Kelley's hand. "Sorry about all of this, how can I help?" Harold asked.

Kelley's first thought, having just been humiliated, was to put Harold face first in the mud where he had just been. He thought about that for more than a few beats before coming to the conclusion that as much as he wanted revenge, revenge was not going to advance his mission. If Harold did not have the drugs and the money, maybe he could help Kelley find out who did.

So they retrieved Kelley's gun and mace, they walked together to Harold's truck. Kelley was dirty and disheveled. Kelley did not like to be dirty and disheveled. It took only a few minutes to find the disk.

Kelley wanted to start by searching the cab of the truck until Harold told him that no one was going to put anything in the cab of his truck without Harold's knowledge. The disk was just lying in the bed of the truck.

"Early yesterday morning were you anywhere near Brownsville, Tennessee?"

"Yes, I was," answered Harold. "I stopped for fuel at a truck stop at exit 42."

Kelley knew exactly where that was. It was a six- hour drive from exactly where he stood. He turned to go and then stopped. He looked back at Harold and thought—there was no way this guy is the perp. But there was no way he was not going to leave until he thoroughly searched Harold's truck.

Harold agreed and even helped with the search, but other than an ice chest full of beer there was nothing of interest to Kelley in the man's truck.

Kelley called his office and ordered them to get the surveillance tapes from every truck stop, gas station and convenience store within one hundred miles of Brownville.

Two officers were dead.

He knew he would have the one tape he actually wanted by the time he got back to Memphis.

As he drove away, Kelley looked back at Harold Hixson. Someday Hixson would be driving through Tennessee and Kelley would make him sorry that he did. He would someday get his revenge. Kelley always won in the end.

As he pulled onto the interstate, he turned on the radio to keep him company on the long trip back to Memphis. Johnny Cash was singing, *"Roughneck"*.

Kelley switched stations. He had had enough of roughnecks.

CHAPTER 13 - *I SAW THE LIGHT.*
Hank Williams
https://www.youtube.com/watch?v=xtolv9kM1qk

Jake hardly slept that Wednesday night and woke up in a cold sweat.

Jen had seemed different and said nothing about the *problem* the night before. Further, Jen had said nothing about their travel plans for the funeral. Was he now worrying about nothing or was there a real problem?

It was early, but Jake called Jen anyhow.

Jen's mother answered.

"This is Jake, is Jen up, can I talk to her?" He asked.

"She's up, but I don't know if she wants to talk to you." He could hear her asking "Jen, do you want to talk to Jake?"

After a pause that was way too long, Jen finally came to the phone. She was crying. "Jake, I'm pregnant." She told him.

The very words Jake had feared.

What to do? What to say?

Jake was not ready for this, not with his father's funeral the very next day.

He took a deep breath and then simply said "I love you, will you marry me?"

Jake was wondering *where that come from.*

It was the best decision he had ever made.

There was silence at the other end of the line. She did love Jake and she could not imagine life without him. Why was there no answer? After an eternity, Jen reluctantly said "Okay."

Jen was not ready to be married, but she liked the idea of having an illegitimate child less.

She had already decided that she would keep the baby no matter what and if Jake refused to grow up, she could divorce him. The fact that she loved Jake was not among the reasons for her assent.

Jake and Jen were married the day after the funeral on May 13th, 1983, in the same church by the same priest. Jake was Methodist, so the big Catholic wedding Jen had often dreamed of was out of the question. Although he did not promise to turn Catholic, Jake did promise his bride a renewal of the vows ceremony with a big reception an unspecified date in the future.

They only had a month left in school so when the newlyweds returned to Baton Rouge, they both graduated on time.

Jake decided he would return to Shreveport to take over the family business. Eloise, Jake's sisters, and the Chandlers all concurred.

Jake's father had several long time employees who could show Jake the ropes. Unfortunately, all of this was decided without consulting with these long time employees nor did the family look at the financial condition of the company.

A month later Jake returned to Shreveport with a pregnant wife to run an unsalvageable business.

Jake Cane would have to grow up in a hurry.

And he needed a miracle.

CHAPTER 14 – *I'LL TAKE THE DOG.*
Jean Shepard and Ray Pillow
https://www.youtube.com/watch?v=GSzSPutEkfE

Jake took Hwy 29 at Hope, Arkansas which turns into Hwy 3 at the Louisiana line. After Jen had thrown him out of their home in the prestigious Pierremont neighborhood, Jake moved into a rental house in Bossier.

He also moved his golf membership to Palmetto Country Club in Benton at Jen's request so that she could continue to enjoy Shreveport Country Club. Benton is on Hwy 3, so Jake stopped at Palmetto for a cheeseburger and a few beers. At Palmetto, a lot of the members had their own golf cart and their own "barn" where they kept their cart.

Jake was lucky enough to buy a used cart from the wife of a member who died and was also able to get his own "barn". When Jake arrived, several members in various states of inebriation were occupying the bar but they soon left for their nearby homes, leaving Jake alone with his beer and Raymond, the bartender, who had been at Palmetto since it opened.

Good bartenders are part friend, part counselor, and mostly listeners. Raymond was a good bartender.

"What's up Jake? Still pining over your ex? You look like you've been rode hard and put up wet." He asked as Jake sat down.

"No, Raymond, just a long drive, took my son off to school. I'm on the way home." He told the bartender.

"Something else is on your mind then? I'm not just looking at tired." Raymond would've never said such a thing if other members were present.

Jake, with nowhere else to go, had often shared his dinner with Raymond in this bar.

They were as close to being friends as a black bartender could be with a rich society boy.

Jake knew that Raymond was smarter and certainly wiser than most of the condescending redneck club members.

Out of curiosity, he asked him, "What would you do if you found a million dollars, Raymond?"

"Find out who it belongs to and give it back to them," was his immediate reply.

"What about the police? Would you call the police?" Jake asked.

"Hell no. You can't trust them bastards to do anything but hit you with a stick. Why? You find something?" The bartender asked him.

"No, just daydreaming." Jake replied.

Raymond sat the beer mug he was drying down on the bar and looked at Jake before speaking, "If someone lost a million dollars, you probably won't have to go looking for them. They'll find you."

As Jake finished his beer in silence, he was thinking, Raymond was probably right. Yet, he was confident no one could trace the lost drugs and money to him. Still, before he left Palmetto, Jake stopped by his barn, re-plugged his golf cart and put an aluminum briefcase and a suitcase in a locker located in the barn.

On his way home, Jake stopped by a friend's house and picked up his dog, Clancy. Everyone in Shreveport and Bossier had a dog, a Lab or some part lab and Jake was no different. Most Labs were black or brown and many were trained retrievers. Some worth thousands of dollars.

But Jake's Lab, Clancy, was unlike the Labs belonging to his friends. He was from a proud and expensive blood line, but he had two strikes against him…he was yellow, and that would not have really been a problem. The real problem with Clancy was that he was gun shy.

Whenever he saw or heard a gun, Clancy would run and hide. So the Cane family got Clancy for nothing. He was a gentle and loyal house dog for the entire family, clearly Jake's favorite member of the family. When Jen threw Jake out, he left nearly everything, but he would not go without Clancy.

Clancy was now over ten years old and had hip problems, he got up slowly and moved slowly, but he was always happy to see Jake.

Jake returned to his dark, lonely house with his best friend Clancy, too tired to do anything but sleep.

Only sleep wouldn't come as he stared at the wall.

As Jake finally drifted off to sleep, his friend Billy lay dying. Jake would not learn of Billy's death for more than twenty-four hours. No one worried when Billy failed to show for work. It was a common occurrence.

CHAPTER 15 - *WELCOME TO MY WORLD.* Jim Reeves
https://www.youtube.com/watch?v=tOCCvN8YDuc

Jake had heard the name before and there were even rumblings that Jake's nickname was in honor of Jacob Goldman. He met Mr. Goldman for the first time at his father's visitation. Mr. Goldman had flown from New York City solely to attend the visitation and the funeral.

While Mr. Goldman and Jake's father were unlikely friends, they were the best of friends nonetheless.

Jacob Goldman looked out of place at his friend's funeral. He was dressed in a dark gray nearly black suit with subtle, almost imperceptible lighter gray stripes. The suit was tailored and fit him perfectly, as did his tailored heavily starched white shirt. He wore a striped Brooks Brothers tie and highly polished cordovan cap toe oxford shoes— probably English, probably made by Church's.

He was a small man with dark piercing eyes and a prominent Jewish nose. His watch was a vintage eighteen karat gold Piaget with a black leather wristband. He had a gold tie tack holding his tie in place with a marquise cut diamond mounted in the center. The man had money but what caught Jake's attention was Goldman's demeanor, kind, caring, concerned and polite. Jacob Goldman was a true gentleman in the best sense.

Jacob Goldman was older than Jake's father but Jacob's exact age, like many other personal details, were never discussed. Jake knew that Jacob was wealthy, that he lived in Manhattan, and in their first meeting Jake had commented, "I think my dad told me that you live in New York?"

To which, Jacob politely replied: "No, I live in Manhattan." And that was that. If Jacob had a job he never discussed it, he had a business card but it only contained his name and a telephone number that was answered by an answering service.

Eventually, Jake would be privy to Jacob's personal number, few were. As a stock broker, Jake was frequently flown to New York by various mutual fund companies and would often dine with Mr. Goldman on those trips. They would always dine alone, but Jacob would often see people he knew and introduce them to Jake. Jake didn't know these people; he just knew who they were: managers of mutual funds, heads of hedge funds, CEOs of major corporations and board members of major corporations.

If Mr. Goldman had a love interest, she was never discussed. Jake and Jacob's conversations usually consisted of talking about investments, companies, stocks, economics and the like. This is not to say that the dinners were tedious or boring. Jacob was a fascinating man and an exceptional conversationalist. Jacob could and did often discuss art and the theater. Jacob seldom went to the opening of a Broadway play, but he never missed a play worth seeing and never missed any significant art exhibit.

On occasion, Jacob would meet Jake at an art opening before dinner. Jacob educated Jake in business matters, theater and to a lesser extent, art. Why Jacob took such an interest in Jake will always remain a mystery as would the basis of the close friendship between Jacob and Jake's father. Jacob Goldman turned out to be the miracle Jake needed a mentor, as well as a friend.

After graduation, Jake and Jen moved in with Eloise in the home built by Jake's grandfather. At least the house was paid for.

Unfortunately, around this time, Jake's Grandma Chandler began 'losing it'. She had the early signs of Alzheimer's and it got worse when Grandpa Chandler had a stroke.

Jake's gravy train abruptly came to an end. The Chandler money would soon be depleted by doctors, hospitals, and nursing homes. Young Jake would soon learn that money is not important if you have it, but when you have no money it becomes extremely important.

Cane Oil & Gas was in worse shape than anyone had imagined. The assets consisted of a tired portfolio of neglected oil and mostly natural gas wells. Some of the wells were marginally profitable, but most were losing money. In fact, the one field with profitable wells was the one field where Jacob Goldman participated.

As he studied the books and the files, Jake learned that Jacob Goldman had been an investor with Cane Oil & Gas as far back as Jake could find records. Unlike many of the prospects, the ones Goldman participated in were mostly successful and profitable. Without those wells, Cane Oil & Gas would have failed long ago. The early eighties were good times for the oil and gas business, but nobody could have saved Cane Oil & Gas and Jake knew he was not equipped with the education, knowledge or experience to be its savior.

Jake's father had friends and one was his outside accountant. Jake first shared what he had learned about the business with Jen and then went to visit the outside accountant.

As Jen had predicted the condition of the company was not news to the accountant. Jake got confirmation of what he already knew and Jen got a part time job.

Jen would later pass the CPA exam on the first try.

It was the accountant who suggested that Jake call Jacob Goldman and it was the accountant that would suggest companies that might be interested in Cane's meager assets.

Since all of his dealings with Jake's father had been profitable, Goldman was a little surprised when he learned the condition of the company and readily agreed to help Jake. After Jake sent the books to Goldman, they followed up with a meeting in New York.

Goldman agreed that the company was beyond saving and Goldman helped Jake with the sale of the assets. With Jen, the accountant and Goldman's counsel and advice, Jake and Eloise were confident and comfortable with what had to be done and moreover what was done, the sale of all assets, the payment of all debts, some at a discount and the avoidance of bankruptcy.

The timing could hardly have been better. Within a few months, the price of oil would drop to ten dollars a barrel and even profitable oil companies would fail.

Jake soon found himself an unemployed, newlywed father, but one who was tougher, more mature, and more focused. Jacob Goldman found Jake a job as a stock broker, all Jake had to do was pass the test. Jake worked harder than he ever had in his life to pass that test, he had to. It is doubtful Jim Reeves was thinking of Jake and Jacob when he sang *"Welcome to my World."*

Had Jake been given to prayer, he would have thanked Jesus for the fact that Jacob Goldman was a part of his world.

CHAPTER 16 - *JAILHOUSE ROCK.*
Elvis Presley
https://www.youtube.com/watch?v=gj0Rz-uP4Mk

D sent Pinky to Louisiana because his three best people were dead or in jail and because he was not about to be personally involved. As far as the rest of the world was concerned, his former employees were rogues and he had nothing to do with whatever activity they had involved themselves in behind D's back.

Or so he had told Kelley's investigators and so his story would remain.

If Pinky got in any trouble, he would claim that he went after the stock broker because of the money he had flashed around at Platinum Plus. D had made that clear and Pinky had reason to obey Big D, to do otherwise would likely be a fatal mistake.

Nevertheless, D was worried about Pinky and instructed Pinky to take Mario with him, someone with no ties to D, and to use a car rented by Mario with cash.

D gave Pinky $1,000 in cash for the trip and two disposable cell phones that would be tossed into the Mississippi River on Pinky's way home to Memphis.

James Cane was not hard to find.

He was in all of the phone books and all over the internet. He even had his home number and address listed in the white pages. Unfortunately, it was an old phone book Pinky found with Jake's old address—Jen's current address.

Mario went to the door and knocked while Pinky waited out front in the car.

No one answered.

The front door was open so Mario waived Pinky away and went inside. Mario had never been in such a spectacular house.

The floors were hardwood covered with oriental rugs. The foyer had an antique demilune table, over which hung an antique mirror with a gold leaf frame. The floor in the foyer was marble, and also covered with an oriental rug.

As he stepped from the foyer into the great room, he could see that the ceilings were over ten feet tall and each wall was covered with original art. Mario was thinking about where he should start his search when the door open and Jen hurried in from a run.

Jen was in running gear wet with sweat, her jog bra and tee shirt did not hide her erect nipples. Even wet with sweat Jen had an aura about her, she was in control and confident, everything Mario hated in a woman.

Mario instantaneously decided that, given the chance, he would fuck this woman and then beat her face in. He was insane and he could just barely control his sick addiction. Before him stood a woman his desire for whom he would not be able to control.

Mario decided no matter what else happened on this trip, he would fuck this rich bitch and then enjoy killing her.

It had taken Jen a few seconds before she realized that she was not alone. By then Mario had grabbed Jen and held a knife to her throat.

"Scream bitch and you die," Jen said nothing, but Mario could feel her tremble and he felt himself getting an erection.

"Where is your husband?" Jen tried to answer, but she was too terrified to talk. Mario took the knife hooked it in the front of Jen's running shorts and cut through the front of the shorts and most of her panties. A trickle of blood ran into Jen's pubic hair from her lower abdomen.

"You going to answer me? Where is your husband?" Jen's knees buckled and she was just about to faint, her mouth would not work.

Finally, Jen blurted out, "My husband doesn't live here. We are separated," And, instantly regretted those words.

This beast now knew that Jen was totally alone.

At least Jen was beginning to think but her thoughts were of her impending rape and death. She could feel Mario's dick harden against her lower back. Just then Mario's phone rang.

"What's going on? Find anything?" Pinky asked.

"Just a sweaty bitch that's about to feel Prince Mario in her ass, best ass I've ever seen." Mario was unzipping his pants. He had already cut the rest of Jen's shorts and panties from her body. Jen screamed and Mario hit her so hard that she fell to the floor semi-conscious.

"No time for that. Where is the stock broker?" Pinky asked as Mario straddled Jen, pinning her arms to the floor with his arms.

Mario's face only inches from Jen's face as he spoke on the phone. Mario said to Jen, "You might as well lay back and enjoy this you are going to get my dick either way."

Mario heard Pinky say, "What did you say? Where is the stock broker?"

"Where is your husband, bitch?" He asked again.

Jen was regaining her consciousness, she was thinking, maybe if I tell him he will leave. Then she wondered *who is he talking to?*

"He lives in Bossier, in Greenacres Subdivision. He's in the phone book under James Cane."

"Pinky, did you hear that?" Mario said into the phone.

"I heard it! Off the bitch and get out here." Pinky told him.

"What if she is lying?" Mario wanted Jen now, but he would wait if he had to. Pinky was out of patience and ready to get out of the neighborhood. He doubted these houses were empty. The wives in these houses didn't work.

"Tie her up. I'll bring the car around back and we'll put her in the trunk; she might prove to be useful."

By now Mario had a raging erection. The more terrified Jen became, the more aroused Mario became. Mario sat up, his pants were open and his dick was nearly in Jen's face. Pre-cum was dripping from Mario onto Jen's chest. She started screaming again and Mario hit her in the face. Her mouth and nose were now bleeding—which excited him even more. Mario flipped Jen on to her stomach and now had an unobstructed view of her ass. Jen kept her figure by running, doing yoga, working out and playing tennis and Jen's adrenaline was at an all-time high. Mario underestimated Jen's strength and when he shifted his weight to pull his pants down further, she bucked him off and sent him sprawling to the floor. Jen was up and headed toward the door before Mario could get to his feet. Unfortunately, she arrived at the door at the exact minute Pinky barged in. Before she could turn, Pinky grabbed her by the right arm and twisted it behind her back.

Jen fainted and pissed all over herself and the Oriental rug by the back door.

This aroused Mario even further, and he was now more determined than ever to have his way with this rich bitch.

"Zip up your pants and go find something to tie her up with." Pinky growled.

"I'm not finished with her, yet."

"Yes you are, we have a job to do and if my boss finds out that you have been wasting his time butt fucking this bitch, he is going to kill us both."

Mario was aroused to the point that he was not going to stop, until he saw Pinky's face. It was a look that had stopped many a fight in Platinum Plus, and it was a look Pinky now supported with a gun pointed right at Mario's chest. To which he replied, "All right but when the job is done, I am going to get a piece of this." Mario pointed at the rich bitch on the floor.

"Get some rope." Pinky demanded.

Pinky found some clothes line and some duct tape in the garage. Jen was tied up still half naked, her mouth taped shut and put into the trunk of the rental.

Pinky and Mario made her fit.

Mario found Jake's address and phone number in a new phone book by Jen's phone. It was midafternoon when they headed across the river to Jake's house.

"Pinky, you gotta admit, that's one hot bitch." Mario told Pinky a little too excited.

"She's kind of old, you pervert."

"Not for me, I'm going to finish with her after we talk to Mr. Stockbroker. Why would he leave a piece like that?" he asked Pinky.

"Probably got caught porking his secretary."

When Pinky reported in to D, he was careful not to mention Mario's extracurricular activities.

Big D was not happy with the report. "You idiot, she knows your names. Talk to the stock broker and don't leave any witnesses. Pinky I want you to search the stockbroker's house and I want you to find out what he knows—and don't park your car anywhere near the house,"

Mario dropped Pinky off at Jake's house and drove to a nearby shopping center. They wouldn't leave a car parked out front to be seen by nosey neighbors. Pinky wouldn't need any help with a pasty stock broker.

It was late afternoon when Pinky broke into Jake's house. Big D said that most people would be at work and he was less likely to be seen. In this neighborhood D was right. More good luck, there was no burglar alarm and the old yellow dog just looked at Pinky and went back to sleep. After searching the house for two hours, Pinky found nothing except for Jake's hunting rifles and shotguns in a gun safe and one suitcase filled with dirty clothes.

No cash, no drugs, and no aluminum briefcase.

Pinky called D on his disposable phone and reported what little he had found. "There is nothing here, hardly any furniture except for a big TV. He has golf clubs lying on the kitchen floor. I don't think this guy has anything except for some hunting guns." He told him.

"Have you talked to him?" Big D asked.

"No, he's not home." Pinky reported.

Jake was D's only lead. "Wait there for him and ask him if he knows anything about the drugs and my money. If you learn anything, let me know. Are you wearing the rubber gloves? Did anyone see you go into the house? Kill the son of a bitch if you have to, but find out if he knows anything."

Pinky was not going back to prison, he was not going to leave any witnesses, and the stock broker was dead one way or the other.

Pinky noticed an old record album on the bookcase. Elvis Presley, *Jail House Rock*. Pinky was not going back to prison, especially Angola.

There would be no witness.

CHAPTER 17 - *MIND YOUR OWN BUSINESS*. Hank Williams
https://www.youtube.com/watch?v=JSeuDDzjIB8

Jake passed the series 7 exam and went to work at the job Jacob had found for him. Friends of Jake's family knew the situation and many entrusted Jake with small amounts of their money. Jacob Goldman transferred one of his accounts to Jake containing nearly $500,000. For the first time in his life, Jake was earning money on his own.

Life at home was also good and the Canes soon had their second child, a son, John Jacob Cane. The first child was a girl, Eloise Paulette Cane. Ellie looked and acted like her mother if anything, even more attractive and more active.

Jen was working part time as a CPA and the Canes were able to move out of the family home and into a small house in the Spring Lake subdivision.

Things would get even better in the fall of 1987 for in September of 1987 Jacob Goldman called Jake and instructed Jake to move all of his money to cash. No reason was given, but Jake did as he was told and asked: "Should I advise my clients to do the same?"

"You can follow my lead with any investment if you wish so long as you first execute my trade," Jacob responded.

Jake was a student of the market. He could see no reason for his friend's action, but by then he knew that Jacob was almost always ahead of the market so Jake advised his other clients to go to cash. The advice was golden, less than a month ahead of "Black Monday", some of his clients took his advice and some did not, by the end of October of 1987 Jake was a star. From that day forward Jake never failed to follow Jacob's lead making his clients and himself financially comfortable, some would say wealthy.

A few years later a lawyer friend of Jake referred Buddy Hawkins. Buddy had seriously injured his leg in an oil field accident and Jake's friend had managed to get him a settlement with the manufacturer of the oil rig in spite of the fact that the accident was most likely the fault of Buddy's employer. After all of the costs, expert fees and attorney's fees were paid, Buddy ended up with about $250,000.00—not nearly enough. In the oil field, Buddy could make $20 to $30 an hour, but was too old and too disabled to make anything like that after his injury.

When people saw Jake and Buddy together, they thought they were brothers, sometimes twins, although Buddy was more than ten years older than Jake. Buddy and Jake were doppelgangers.

Buddy was an interesting man, but he rarely read anything except for gun, motorcycle and car magazines. He could fix anything and seemed to know everything about guns. With two good legs, Buddy could have probably worked as a mechanic but he worked too slowly and anything Buddy did had to be done right and to Buddy that meant perfect. Perfect is a lofty but unattainable goal so Buddy nearly always took too long with his projects.

Jake shared Buddy's interest in cars but not so much Buddy's obsession with guns. Buddy was the best shot Jake had ever seen. He could kill more squirrels with a twenty-two rifle than anyone else could with a twelve gauge shotgun.

In addition to his settlement, Buddy received a small Social Security disability check and another check from a military disability. Jake knew this and that Buddy had been in the military where he had been discharged after his injury.

Buddy had medals, but he never talked about his military past at all. Jake thought that Buddy had been in the military at the tail end of the Vietnam War but if anyone knew it was never discussed.

Buddy was not the type of client Jake sought. There is little money for a stock broker in a two-hundred and fifty thousand dollar account. But, Buddy had something few of Jake's other friends possessed, genuineness. What you see is what you got with Buddy. If Buddy liked you, it did not matter who your parents were, what school you went to, or how much money you had in your bank account. None of those things mattered.

Buddy liked Jake and the feeling was mutual. As a bonus, Buddy liked classic country music and always had it playing in his shop. Over the years that followed, Buddy would become Jake's best friend.

Nearly every Tuesday after work Jake would stop by Buddy's shop with a six pack of beer and they would talk about cars, motorcycles, music, women, guns and sometimes sports. Other characters would often be present at these confabs. It was a different group from Jake's norm, a group Jake enjoyed more than his regular social circle. Buddy and Jake hunted together and both loved cars. Buddy had a gun dealer's license and had quite a collection of exotic weapons.

Jake could be himself around Buddy and Buddy's friends. None of those people were the least bit interested in Jake's business and would not abide anyone who tried to get into theirs.   Anytime gossip began to make its way into a conversation in Buddy's shop, Buddy would play Hank Williams singing *Mind Your Own Business*, and the conversation always took a different turn.

CHAPTER 18 - *HELLO WALLS.*
Faron Young
https://www.youtube.com/watch?v=HMSWAUAKJn0

Jake had been out of his office for several days and he had to work late to catch up. He'd answered most of his calls in route to his office, so most of what Jake did that day was paperwork.

He stopped by the Shreveport Club for dinner alone before heading home. It was after eight and almost dark when he finally arrived home.

Jake opened the garage and parked his pearl white Police Interceptor in the garage next to his old fishing truck—actually the truck Jake's father had owned when he was killed.

Tonight would be spent with Faron Young as his only company. Jake was anticipating a long night talking to the walls, windows and staring up at the ceiling. Faron Young had been a favorite of Jake's father and now Willie Nelson was one of his.

Jake was worn out from the travel and a full day of work. He had been so busy that he had hardly been able to give much thought to the money and the drugs. He should have noticed that someone had been through the boxes of junk in his garage, but he didn't.

The door to the house from the garage was always left open so it was not unusual for it to be unlocked. Jake walked in, turned on the light, and instantly felt the barrel of Pinky's gun on his lower back.

"You Jake Cane?" a man's voice asked.

"Yes, what do you want?" Jake amazed himself with how calm he was. He knew exactly what this man wanted—and he should have been terrified.

"You got something that belongs to my boss and he wants it back." Pinky escorted Jake into the living room with the gun in his hand and turned on the lights with his other.

Every bit of Jake's furniture was turned upside down and inside out and every cabinet he could see in the kitchen had been emptied.

"I don't know what you are talking about. It looks like you already know that I don't have anything here that belongs to your boss." Why, Jake thought, did you say "here"? Maybe this guy didn't catch Jake's mistake.

Just as Clancy was getting up to greet Jake, he saw the gun, and quickly turned tail and retreated to the safety of his bed.

It took Pinky a few beats to process what Jake had said, but he did. "Okay, where did you hide the money and the drugs?"

"What money and drugs? I don't know what you are talking about." Jake was no longer calm. Sweat began to collect under his arms and on his brow, and his knees were weak and began to shake. Pinky turned Jake around and gave him his "look."

Jake knew he was going to die.

Jake's mind was spinning. *Think you fool, if you tell him what he wants to know you are certainly dead.*

"Where is the stuff? I'm going to find out one way or another."

He was barely able to talk much less think, but Jake got the words out, "If I had what you want I would give it to you. I don't want any trouble."

"Well mister you got you some trouble, you're lying. And I will get what I want." Pinky grabbed Jake's arm like he had done with Jen earlier and forced Jake into his bedroom, intending to force Jake's head into the toilet.

Pinky knew that Jake had the goods. He was going to find out where they were hidden. Jake involuntarily cried out in pain. Pinky was about to dislocate Jake's shoulder and it was not by accident. As they crossed the bedroom Jake heard a growl come from Clancy.

It was a sound Jake had never heard in the previous ten plus years of Clancy's life. Pinky had put his gun in the front of his pants and was using both hands to escort Jake to the bathroom. He'd turned just as Clancy jumped at Pinky, fangs bared and destined for Pinky's neck. Pinky let go of Jake and put his arm up just in time to be hit by the full force of Clancy's eighty pounds.

Pinky was knocked to the floor with Clancy's mouth locked on his left arm. Clancy started shaking back and forth with his whole body in an effort to separate Pinky's arm from his body.

It was Pinky that was now crying out in pain.

Jake did not like to have guns around, especially loaded guns. His dad had always taught Jake that all guns are dangerous and that all guns should be treated as loaded. Even though he no longer had an angry wife and young children around, he still kept his guns unloaded and locked up.

Jake was wishing that he had ignored this piece of his Dad's advice. What Jake did keep for defense was one of his son's aluminum baseball bats. He kept the bat under his bed in plain view from where he now laid on the floor.

He'd never intended to use the bat on an intruder with a gun, but it was all he had—so he grabbed the bat just in time to hear the gun shot that would kill Clancy.

As Clancy died, his grip on Pinky's left arm relaxed.

Pinky was looking at his mangled left arm when the bat smashed into his right forearm breaking both bones. The gun fell from Pinky's hand at about the same time as the bat crashed into the right side of Pinky's face.

CHAPTERS 19 - *LIVE FAST, LOVE HARD, DIE YOUNG.* Faron Young
https://www.youtube.com/watch?v=PrIblTLbPVM

With his own hard work, dumb luck, and tips from Jacob Goldman, Jake was the most successful stock broker in Shreveport. He turned down any account of less than half a million dollars and most of his accounts contained seven figures, with a few accounts containing eight. He was now a vice president of the firm and was strong enough to pretty much make his own rules.

He was also strong enough to turn down any client who was the least bit shady or demanding.

Jake was a straight arrow and he was not about to do anything that had the slightest hint of impropriety. Eloise was exceedingly proud of her son.

The Cane and Chandler names had been restored to their past glory by Jake Cane.

True people of Shreveport society do not flaunt their wealth; they have been known to drive a Chevy to the hangers where they keep their private jet. Jake wanted a big BMW or a Porsche, but Eloise cautioned against such an ostentatious display of wealth. "What would people think?" On the other hand, Jen *was not from here*. And she was free to drive whatever she wanted to drive.

Jen got the Lexus SUV and Jake got a Ford.

After many years of driving Fords, Jake got to know the owner of the local Ford dealership well. In fact, the Ford dealer and his family were some of Jake's better clients. One fall when Jake went to trade for a new Ford, he saw the Police Interceptor in the back of the lot. "Who is that going to?" Jake asked.

"Arcadia ordered it but some business shut down and they don't have the money to pay for it. It's for sale. I may have it sold to a little town in east Texas." The car dealer told him.

Jake was thinking, "What if I bought this and fixed it up? I could have a Ford that could outrun a BMW."

"Hold it for a few days, I might be interested." Jake told the dealer.

The next Tuesday Jake, Buddy, and a few others drank beer and talked about the Interceptor. Jake left Buddy's house and drove straight to the dealership and bought the car.

A few months later the Interceptor was supercharged. It was custom painted pearl white metallic and had a custom interior of tufted brown supple leather. There may have been faster BMWs, but it is doubtful that there was a faster or more luxurious Ford anywhere.

Buddy loved the car. He would always ask Jake how the "Corinthian" leather was holding up. The car was a 2001 model; it was Jake's fortieth birthday present from Jake, to Jake. Was middle age crazy setting in?

The Interceptor was the first "wild" thing Jake had done since he married Jen. He still loved his wife and if anything Jen became more beautiful with age. The scar on her chin had faded and was now expertly covered with makeup. After being hit in the nose by a tennis ball the best plastic surgeon had fixed Jen's nose for free—it was his wife who had hit Jen in the nose. Most of her accent was now gone, except during visits to Chalmette and she was fully accepted by Shreveport society. Those who did not know just assumed that Jen was from an old Shreveport family and those that knew that she was from New Orleans assumed that she grew up in the Garden District. Nor had their love life gone stale. The Canes frequently went alone to Europe and to the Caribbean and truly enjoyed each other.

The only part of Faron Young's song Jake was living was his hot rod car. Some secretly loathed the Canes.

Nobody deserves to be that perfect.

CHAPTER 20 - *I'LL NEVER GET OUT OF THIS WORLD ALIVE.* Hank Williams
https://www.youtube.com/watch?v=w7FQeFOBtBk

Pinky was on the floor of Jake's bedroom lying next to Clancy wrapped up in duct tape like a mummy.

Clancy was dead and Pinky was close.

There was no way Pinky could move. His left arm burned, ached, and stung where he had been bitten by the dog. His right arm throbbed, as did the right side of his face.

Pinky had dished out a lot of pain in his life—but he'd never felt pain like this. He could hardly maintain consciousness.

He was past worried and pretty sure he was going to die; Jake was nowhere to be seen.

After Jake had wrapped Pinky up, he rifled through his pockets and found a wallet, a cell phone, and a wad of cash.

The man's name was Sidney Jones. He lived in Memphis on a street Jake did not recognize. Sidney was twenty-seven years old.

Pinky was still out when Jake slipped out of his back door to look for Sidney's car. He looked over as much of the neighborhood as he could while saying out of sight. Jake saw no unusual vehicles and was about to give up, when he spotted a nondescript late model Nissan driving slowly up the street toward Jake's house.

It was another dark cloudy, moonless night. Jake's backyard was darker still, due to the large Bradford Pear tree that shaded the back of his house.

The tree frogs and crickets provided the only noise.

The motion light in the driveway would light up if a car or a person were to venture up Jake's driveway. He retreated to his back yard.

If this was Sidney's accomplice he would come up the driveway and try to get into the house through the back yard so as not to be seen. At least, that is what

Jake figured, and he would be waiting in the shadow of that pear tree with Sidney's loaded gun and his son's baseball bat.

Mario was worried—Pinky wasn't answering his phone and it had been more than an hour. The stock broker would surely be home by now. Mario turned into the driveway.

The motion light came on, temporarily blinding him, and when he was able to see again, he saw the gate into the back yard and hurried through. He never saw Jake swing the bat that crushed his right knee cap nor did he anticipate the blow to the back of his head. Jake drug Mario into his kitchen, this time he fastened Mario's hands together with some plastic straps the cable installer had left last week.

What else could he do? Jake was no good with knots and the duct tape was gone. This would prove to be a fatal mistake.

Mario was not as big as Pinky and Jake was able to prop him up in a chair in the kitchen. He had barely finished searching Mario's pockets when Mario slowly regained consciousness. Jake was inspecting the items he had found. A switchblade knife, Jake had never actually seen one of those, two guns, one found in Mario's pants pocket and one in his left boot, car keys, the keys were for a rental, and a diamond ring.

What is this diamond ring doing in this guy's pocket? Jake wondered and then it hit him: this is Jen's ring.

First fear and then rage coursed through Jake's body.

Mario jerked back and Pinky winced visibly at the look on Jake's face as he demanded, "Where is my wife?"

Pinky's mouth was taped shut, he could not answer.

Mario regained his composure and said, touting, "Was that your wife with the fabulous ass? I am going to finish with her when we are done here." His hands were suddenly free and he lunged at Jake apparently forgetting that his right leg was not going to work. The gun in Jake's right hand discharged, the bullet hit Mario in his left eye and blew out the back part of his head.

In an instant, Prince Mario lay dead, literally at Jake's feet.

Jake will swear to this day that he never meant to fire.

Jake will claim that the gun must have had a hair trigger, or that Mario must have accidently discharged the gun when he tried to grab Jake. But, at that moment, Pinky could not have thought that what he had witnessed was an accidental shooting.

Jake did not react at all except to kick Mario away from his feet and then turn the gun towards Pinky's head.

As he tore the tape from Pinky's mouth Jake said, again.

"Where is my wife?"

CHAPTER 21- *ALMOST PERSUADED or SUZIE Q.* David Houston; Dale Hawkins
https://www.youtube.com/watch?v=ZKmVgaqmRFQ
https://www.youtube.com/watch?v=N0L44Zea9Ms

In May of 2003, Jake and Jen would celebrate their twentieth wedding anniversary with a ceremony at First Methodist Church presided over by the Methodist pastor and by a Catholic Monsignor and followed by a huge party at Shreveport Country Club.

Jen had become even more attractive as she aged, her hair required color, but her body was just a firm as ever. Ellie was better looking than her mother and a junior at Ole Miss and their son, Jacob would start William & Mary in the fall.

The Canes were the toast of Shreveport. Jake and Jen had to be careful that they not leave anyone off of the invitation list...even his friend Buddy made the list.

Buddy did not go to the church service, but he did make an appearance at the reception. Jake saw Buddy and made it a point to talk to him.

Buddy looked a bit uncomfortable: "Buddy, thanks for coming. How did you enjoy your time in church?" Jake was fairly certain that Buddy did not spend a lot of his time in church.

"I missed church. I did not want to encourage those people. If you ask me there are too many God damn churches in this town and not enough Christians." The next time Jake looked, Buddy was gone.

Jake was the past president of the Kiwanis Club, past president of Shreveport Country Club, a Holiday and Dixie Diplomat and on the board of the Chamber of Commerce.

Jen was past president of the Junior League, the Shreveport Arts Council and on the Board of the Shreveport Opera and The Strand.

Ellie had her turn as Queen of the Cotillion.

Then came the summer of 2003.

The summer started just like every summer before. His clients were still a bunch of rich, paranoid crybabies who panicked with every downturn in the market. In spite of the fact that Jake had, for the most part, made them rich was in the past. Every day was a new day and the unspoken message was: *what have you done for me lately, or more to the point...what have you done for me today?*

His promotion to Vice President increased his compensation and prestige, but also created a whole new set of problems—managing a staff. Jake was now expected to listen to the infernal whining from a bunch of spoiled overpaid brokers, their assistants, and the mistreated secretarial staff. On top of that Jen had quit her job, the kids were almost grown and she was finding things to complain about just because she had too much time.

Jen played tennis, went to yoga, had lunch with her many friends and then complained when Jake was too tired to go out at night. Jake endured, they never really fought and there were none of the makeup sex sessions of the past.

If not for her running, where Jake sometimes joined her, the "perfect" life of the Canes was turning into the same old rut.

Jake was bored and his hot-rod Ford was no remedy.

Jake first saw Suzie standing in the hall talking to the office manager. She had pale skin with an innocent face, lightly sprinkled with freckles. Her breasts were prominently displayed in the light pink shift she wore. She had a small nose and mouth and soft, childlike features. Her hair was strawberry blond and cut to shoulder length. She was no more than five feet four and at least ten years younger than Jake could not have weighed much more than 100 pounds. She looked good but no better than dozens of women who had come on to Jake in the past.

Women liked money and power and Jake had both, but he loved his wife, feared his mother and had always politely brushed off or ignored any advances from other women. Such that he was never sure if they were advances but more importantly to Jake, no one got hurt. Had Jake been more observant the day he met Suzie, he might have noticed that this innocent young girl wore heels that were half an inch too tall and the hem of her shift was an inch too high. And had he studied her resume a little closer, he would have noticed the quick promotions followed by early departures.

He might have noticed that her breasts were unusually large for a person of her size, as well. But none of these clues registered.

What he did notice was that Suzie's shift had a zipper in the front with a key ring attached to the pull. Jake could not stop thinking about what it would be like to tug on that zipper and to drop that dress off of those young creamy white shoulders.

A few days later Jacob Goldman died suddenly in New York. To Jake, the death was sudden because the man had kept the fact that he had pancreatic cancer a secret. Jake was despondent for weeks, uncharacteristically moody and short with his family, co-workers, and friends.

A week later Buddy said: "What's up your ass? You lose a leg? Nobody wants to hear your whining." Jake instantly felt better.

Buddy had that effect on people.

A few days later, Eloise fell down the stairs and broke her hip. Although she would eventually recover, the surgery, medications and her advancing years led Jake to believe that she was going the way of his grandma Chandler. It sure seemed like Alzheimer's and helpful friends and clients were quick to remind Jake of a mother, aunt, or grandmother, who had broken their hip and never recovered.

It did not help when Eloise was forced into a rehab facility when she was released from the hospital.

Soon Suzie was employed by Jake's firm and he saw her daily.

Most of Suzie's clothes were subtly suggestive and once every couple of weeks the pink shift with the zipper in front would show up. Each time the zipper seemed to be pulled a little lower exposing ever more cleavage. For the first time in twenty years, Jake was interested in another woman and every signal from Suzie indicated that she was interested in Jake.

One Tuesday after work Jake skipped his trip to Buddy's and instead went with a group, including Suzie, to happy hour at the Blind Tiger. Suzie wore the pink shift exposing the tops of her freckled breasts as she sat demurely across from Jake. Occasionally Suzie would bend over to get something from her purse or to pick up her napkin from the floor. When she did, he would catch a glimpse of the pink circles around Suzie's nipples.

Jake could observe that the color of Suzie's nipples nearly matched the color of her dress. Before long everyone was gone except for Jake and Suzie and before too much longer Jake and Suzie were together in a room across the river at the Horseshoe Casino.

It was all too easy and for the first time in years Jake felt a desire he thought was lost. The feeling was pure lust but it was a feeling he missed, and he now remembered how much he liked that feeling.

Jake forgot to remember the lesson of David Houston's *Almost Persuaded* probably the most popular Classic country song of all time. Unlike Jake, the husband in *Almost Persuaded* resisted temptation and went home to his wife. At this point in his life, Jake could resist anything but temptation, and the temptress Suzie was irresistible to him and as he would later learn, too many before him.

Looking back later, Jake would realize that Suzie got her kicks from destroying men like Jake. Suzie's innocent good looks gave her power over men who are after all the weaker sex. Suzie got her kicks taking advantage of that weakness.

Jen knew something was up, and she might have ignored it until it went away if not for the fact that Jake saw fit to take Suzie to New York for a weekend paid for by one of the mutual fund companies. There in New York while at a romantic dinner with Suzie, Jake ran into three couples in from Shreveport for a play. All of the couples were friends and one of the men was a co-worker of Jake. Jake received the call from Jen before the night was over. It did not help and it was probably no accident that Suzie could be heard talking in the background while Jake tried to explain.

Jake came home to a wife wielding a shotgun.

Suzie was fired on Monday.

Jake was called to the home office for a sit-down meeting with several of his company's executives. If not for Jake's portfolio of business he would have also been fired.

Jake would lose a few clients, but he was still a star and the fact that he earned money for his clients and even larger sums of money for his employer allowed his employer to bend rules that would have doomed a lesser producer.

Jake's life would be different now, had he only been *Almost Persuaded* by *Suzie Q*.

CHAPTER 22 - *I CAN'T HELP IT (IF I AM STILL IN LOVE WITH YOU).*
Hank Williams
https://www.youtube.com/watch?v=ax0Lsl3MvIk

Jake opened the trunk of the car and found Jen. She was alive, her eyes at first displaying terror which gradually turned to relief and then to anger. Blood had coagulated around her nose and the tape covering her mouth. Jake tore the tape from Jen's mouth and used Mario's knife to cut the clotheslines from her hands and feet.

As he helped Jen from the trunk, he could see the cut on her lower abdomen and the blood in her pubic hair.

The men in Jake's family do not cry, but tears welled up in Jake's eyes and ran down his cheeks. Jen allowed Jake to hold her and to help her into the house. Once inside, Jen sat on a kitchen chair and blankly stared at the dead Mario and the mummified Pinky, who were both lying on the kitchen floor. Jake found a pair of jogging pants for Jen to wear.

"I never thought anything like this would happen," Jake said. Jen had no idea what Jake had done or for that matter, what had happened. She was still in shock. "You know I would never intentionally do anything to hurt you."

Jen was silent, just now realizing that she was not going to die.

"If that's true why do I keep getting hurt? Who are these men?" She looked again at Mario and saw for the first time that the back of his head was missing. Jen would later confess that she felt no remorse for Mario, only relief…or was it satisfaction? "What happened to him?" She asked.

"I shot him. And I am going to do the same with that other piece of shit lying next to him." Jake had not enjoyed shooting Mario and he did not want to shoot Pinky or anyone else. Jake only knew that Pinky worked for someone who wanted what Jake had and was willing to kill to get it back. Jake needed to find out who that person was. He was ready to give back the money and the drugs. Things were again failing to go as planned, probably because had no plan. Jake had begun to formulate a plan and part of Jake's plan was to make Pinky believe that he had two choices, name his boss or die.

Jen spoke first. "You don't need to shoot him, he can't hurt you now." Actually, at that moment, if truth be known, she would have happily shot Pinky herself.

"Yes, he can. He saw me shoot that other guy and he knows that I have something he wants."

"We need to call the police and let them sort this out."

"I might as well kill him first. They can only execute me once." Jen's head was spinning, that dead son of a bitch had tried to rape her and intended to rape her and then kill her. He got just what he deserved, how could Jake be in trouble for killing that perverted beast?

"Help me wrap the bastard up. I need to get his dead body out of my house." Still dazed Jen pulled the cover off of Jake's bed and helped him put the body in the back of his old truck. Jake carefully wrapped

Clancy in an old blanket and put him in the back of the truck with Mario's body.

Once they were out of Pinky's hearing range, Jake told Jen what he had done. Jen could not believe how far her former *perfect* husband had fallen. Her Catholic guilt made her wonder if she had not herself been in part, the cause of his fall.

Maybe she should have forgiven Jake, as her father had told her and as Eloise had begged her to do. It was too late for forgiveness now and having just escaped rape and death do to Jake's bad choices, Jen was absolutely not in the mood to forgive him now. On the other hand, she did still have feelings for Jake and the business side of Jen realized that Jake was the father of her children and for the most part still the provider for her children. Jake in prison could not be good for the family. Moreover, that son of a bitch in the back of Jake's truck needed killing.

"Take my car and get out of here. Go to your father's house, they will be looking for my car." Jen's response cut Jake to the core. "I'll be all right. I'll go to Joe's house. They won't look for me there." Jake said nothing as he watched Jen drive away. 'Joe the Grinder' is what Jake called him; maybe he would shoot that vulture too.

CHAPTER 23 - *IT WASN'T GOD WHO MADE HONKY TONK ANGELS.*
Kitty Wells
https://www.youtube.com/watch?v=tKleTa94dC8

Jake had been on top of the world and he was confident that Jen would forgive him and let him come home. Especially since Jen's father had cursed Jake out as only a longshoremen could, but had forgiven Jake and told Jen to do the same.

Jake was willing to take his punishment. He was sure enough of himself to think that Jen could not live without him. Jen might have taken him back if he had just behaved himself, but he did not. Instead, Jake engaged in several dalliances (that is how he thought of them), with a few willing divorcees.

As long as Jake continued that type of behavior, no amount of pleading by Eloise was going to soften Jen's resolve.

What is good for the goose is good for the gander and so it was that Jen eventually accepted a dinner invitation from Joseph Hawkins. Joe was a former college running back and the son of a wildly successful oil man. Unlike Jake's father, Joe had taken over his father's business and had, by all appearances, made it even more successful. Jake had invested in several of Joe's prospects and had made money on all of them.

Joe had been married, but not for long. He was nearly six feet tall, with the broad shoulders of a former athlete. He was confident and could be charming and personable when he wanted to be.

Over the years, he had developed a belly, and he had been known to brag in the petroleum club that, "If you've got a good tool, you build a shed over it."

Joe's once dark hair was graying, wavy and thinning in the back. Nonetheless, Joe was a catch. He knew it and took full advantage.

He also knew how women like to be treated, from a lot of experience. After a few too many drinks Joe would also say, "I envy you married guys. As soon as I get tired of strange pussy and my own spending money I plan to get married myself."

Joe showered Jen with appropriate and thoughtful gifts, took her to all of the right places and parties and soon had Jen spending nights in his bed. If Jen felt guilty, she never showed it. What girl doesn't like being treated like a movie star, which is exactly how Joe treated Jen. The Canes had not filed for divorce, but Jen was now giving that option some thought. Jen ignored comments from her friends about Joe; she knew that she was different than all of the women Joe had bedded in the past.

When Jake picked his son up for the trip to college, he knew that Jen would be staying with Joe. The thought made Jake sick to his stomach. Jake had never liked Joe much and he now hated Joe's guts. Logic said that Jake had caused his own problems. Jake wanted to blame them on Joe.

John barely talked to his father on the trip to Virginia. Neither of Jake's children talked to him any more than was absolutely necessary. As the Cane children saw their world, Jake had hurt their mother and destroyed their family because their father was no different than the grandfather they had only heard about.

To Jake's children, he was a worthless no account womanizer. The trip to Virginia had been misery for both Jake and his son.

As he drove through Tennessee after Jake dropped his son off at college, he heard Kitty Wells' *It Wasn't God Who Made Honky Tonk Angels*. Jake called Jen on his cell phone. She answered. He could tell Joe was present. Jake said only: "John is safely in his dorm."

"Good," was all she said. When the conversation was over, Jake's stomach hurt. Several hours later Jake would stop to relieve himself outside of Brownsville, Tennessee.

CHAPTER 24 - *SETTING THE WOODS ON FIRE.* Hank Williams
https://www.youtube.com/watch?v=F3hzYRVAkUs

Jake ripped the tape from Pinky's mouth.

"I am going to ask one time and if I do not get a straight answer, I am going to shoot you in the right eye and put you down the well with your dead friend. Who sent you here?" He asked.

Pinky was a believer.

"Dan Stephens, they call him Big D. He owns Platinum Plus and a construction company in Memphis." Jake took a second to process the man's answer.

It made perfect sense—the guy was probably telling the truth.

Jake had the two cell phones, one of them rang. Jake showed the phone to Pinky before asking, "Who is calling?"

"That's D."

Jake answered the phone.

"Hello Big D. This is Jake Cane, and I've got something you want. I want to give you what I have, if you leave me alone."

D did not answer.

Instead the line went dead.

Jake cut enough tape off of Pinky so that he could move. Pinky was not much of a threat with a mangled right arm and a torn opened left arm and his only hope was to get away with his life.

"You see that rifle in my gun case?" Jake pointed to his Weatherly Mark 5 rifle with a Zeiss Conquest Scope.

Pinky knew that rifle would do the job.

"Go tell Big D that I know who he is and that I know where he lives. Tell him that I will give him back what he wants, but if anyone else comes looking for me I will lay in wait for him with that rifle and I will kill him." He paused for a moment so that Pinky could think about what he said.

"Do you understand?"

"Uh huh." Pinky responded.

"Is that a YES?"

"Yes." He said.

Jake put the keys to the rental car in Pinky's left hand. Jake kept all of the guns, the two cell phones, and the knife. "Get out of here and don't look back."

Within seconds, Pinky was gone.

Jake and Jen cleaned up the kitchen and put the bloody towels in a bag in the back of Jake's truck. They had straightened up the house up as well, but any trained observer would notice that things were out of place.

A careful observer would know that the house had been searched and that someone had been injured in the kitchen.

Jake knew that someone else was looking for him, but he was confident that they did not know who he was, after all how could they? Big D was not going to tell them.

It was near midnight when Jake left home and drove his old pickup truck north on Airline Drive toward Benton. On the trip, he passed by the country club where the money and drugs were hidden. From Benton, he took Highway 162 to 7 Pines Road and then north to the hunting camp. It was after midnight when he arrived at the camp. No one was there as deer season would not start for several weeks. Jake had a particular destination in mind, an old abandoned well at least a half a mile off of any road. When hunting club members shot a deer, they would usually dress it and leave the innards on the ground for the coyotes and other varmints to clean up.

Same with a hog just leave it and everything but the bones would be gone in days. Sometimes the kill was too close to the camp and to avoid the smell and the unwanted scavengers the hunter's would take their kill to this old well, dump it down the well and cover it with acid. Prince Mario along with poor old Clancy, were now headed for the same fate.

It was not easy for Jake to load Mario onto the Rhino to transport his body to the well. He had to make a second trip with Clancy and the acid left over from last year. An hour later Mario and Clancy had been laid to rest and were in the process of being dissolved.

Jake hated to do that to Clancy, but he did not have time for anything else, nor did he have an explanation for how Clancy got shot. When Jen told him what Mario had done to her, Jake had felt no remorse.

Back at the camp Jake scrubbed himself clean, changed into some clothes he had brought from home and headed back to town. On the way, he stopped by Palmetto and picked up the money and the drugs. Jake had to figure out how he could get the money and drugs back to its owners and to stay alive doing so.

It was 2:30 in the morning by the time Jake turned into his subdivision.

He was dead tired. The adrenalin had long since worn off.

Nothing was moving on his street. He was worried that he might see a patrolling cop car and was thinking about what he would say if stopped. At least he was sober; most men out at this late hour probably were not.

Nothing looked out of order on Jake's street considering the fact that a murder had taken place on this very street only a few hours earlier. The fact that nothing was out of order was a happy surprise to him.

But just as a precaution, Jake decided to drive around his block.

Something felt wrong as he passed his house.

Did he see a moving light inside? If so, it went out as he passed.

Jake passed his house and turned at the next corner. He was not as familiar with this block, but he was certain that he had never before seen a black SUV parked there. The closer he got the more he realized that this out of place black Tahoe looked familiar. This black Tahoe looked remarkably similar to a black Tahoe he had seen a few days earlier in a vacant lot in Brownsville, Tennessee. This black Tahoe even had Tennessee plates. The only discernable difference was the fact that the plates on this black Tahoe were public plates.

This black Tahoe was property of the state of Tennessee.

Jake first felt the sensation of blood draining out of his head. He almost fainted. The next sensation was one of adrenaline coursing through his veins.

Suddenly, Jake was wide awake. What to do now? He had not yet gotten away with his first murder. One murder was enough for Jake, even if Mario needed killing.

Was God playing some cruel trick on Jake? Was the existence of this truck in this place a mere coincidence?

Not likely. He was now certain that someone was in his house when he passed. More of Big D's thugs? Not Likely.

There had only been a few hours since Jake had talked to D and he would not be in a vehicle with public plates, would he? Jake could not park anywhere without himself being conspicuous.

He was not cut out for this—any of this.

CHAPTER 25 - *IT'S FOUR IN THE MORNING.* Faron Young

https://www.youtube.com/watch?v=Ml3MJfr_wXQ

Kelley saw the whole thing on the video his people got from the truck stop. He was barely able to see the Louisiana license plate on Jake's car, but was able to decipher enough letters and numbers to zero in on the one Ford Interceptor with all of the discernible letters and numbers.

The car belonged to James S. Cane.

Cane had lived in Shreveport, Louisiana, but had recently moved to Bossier. He had three vehicles, a Lexus LX 470, a 1982 Ford F-150 pickup truck and the Interceptor. Cane was a stock broker and Kelley could find no reason why he would have a police car. Cane had no criminal record. The website of Jake's firm contained several photos of Jake Cane. He didn't look like a thief or murderer, but Kelley knew all too well that criminals come in all shapes and sizes. Kelley did think that he could tell if a man was dangerous and Cane did not look like a dangerous man. Kelley could find no clues as to why such a man would be involved in the murder of four men and the theft of Kelley's money and drugs.

Kelley intended to get answers.

Kelley wanted his money, but what he really needed was the drugs he had borrowed from the evidence room. Before long those drugs were going to turn up missing and the list of people who have access to those drugs was short. Kelley was hopped up on bennies the entire trip from Memphis to Shreveport. No lights were on at Cane's house when Kelley arrived in the early morning hours. Kelley parked on the street behind Cane's house and quietly made his way over the fence behind the house. Kelley was not in uniform, but he had identification and could claim to be working undercover if he got caught. No one saw Kelley and no one heard him. Nothing in Cane's background gave Kelley any reason to fear Cane, but with four dead and one injured, Kelley assumed that there was something about this Cane that did not show up in any database. That is not to say that Kelley was afraid, far from it, cautious is a better word.

Kelley had no trouble with the sliding glass door in the back of the house. Kelley quietly and carefully searched every room and found no one. No cars in the garage. The house smelled of Lysol and death. Kelley could see that someone had recently searched the house and he could sense that a struggle had taken place with gunfire involved. There remained a faint smell of gunpowder. Some brain tissue on the baseboard in the kitchen. Kelley knew that a forensic investigator could tell him a lot more, but Kelley did not have that luxury. Who had searched the house? Where were they? Where was Cane? Was it Cane's brain tissue? Had someone else already found Cane and did someone else have Kelley's money and drugs?

Kelley was not a worrier—he was a doer. He made other people worry, but the thoughts creeping into Kelley's head could only be classified as worry. Was he at a dead end? All he could do was wait. He was not good at waiting and at 4:00 am he gave up and left, this time by the front door.

Jake parked his truck in the parking lot of a nearby condominium development. He was so far away that he could just barely see the Tahoe. It was

4:00 am when the lights on the Tahoe came on and it began driving down the boulevard.

Jake hunkered down among a hedge of azaleas near a condo, and when the Tahoe passed under a street light, Jake was not totally surprised to see Kelley at the wheel. Jake stayed perfectly still until the Tahoe turned onto Benton Road toward town.

Jake stayed still several minutes longer before making his way back to the truck.

What now? Before Jake could answer his own question, the Tahoe appeared from the south and turned back into the subdivision. Jake followed the path of the Tahoe as it turned down his street and appeared to slow. As soon as the Tahoe was out of sight, Jake was out of the subdivision and on his way to Shreveport.

There was only one place he could go at four in the morning. Buddy would be awake, drinking coffee. It was four in the morning, but Jake was not experiencing the feelings Faron Young had sung about, far from it. Jake wished he had made better choices. A fool, period.

CHAPTER 26 - *PICK ME UP ON YOUR WAY DOWN.* Webb Pierce
https://www.youtube.com/watch?v=vS2WZda89N8

Jen called Joe before she reached the I-20 Bridge and he sounded asleep and groggy. Jen was certain that she heard a female voice in the background when Joe answered the phone. She was sick.

Not again?

"Who is that?" She asked.

"No one is here. That's the TV. I fell asleep with the TV on." Jen again heard a voice in the background and it did not sound like TV. "Why are you calling at this time of the night, is something wrong?"

"Yes, I need to stay at your house for a few days." Silence and more silence, then:

"Not now, my daughter is coming with the grandchildren to stay for a few days." This was the first time Joe had ever mentioned his grandchildren.

That faint sleepy voice again in the background.

"Who is there with you?" Silence, then Jen hung up. She wanted to be hurt. She wanted to be surprised. But she was neither.

There is only one good man in this world, Paul Richard. Jen would go to Chalmette. Jen did not cry. She would no longer allow herself to cry over worthless men.

A Webb Pierce CD was playing on Jake's radio. Jen claimed to hate Webb Pierce, saying when he sang, it sounded nasal and whiny. She hated the fiddles and the honky tonk piano.

She looked for the button that would stop the noise, but she didn't look hard. Strangely, the sound of Webb Pierce was somehow soothing and if Jen needed anything, she needed comfort from somewhere. She could not admit it but she missed this simple, stupid music and she missed her piece of shit husband.

She had never seen him cry, not when his father died, not when his grandparents died, not when he had tripped and broken his arm and not when his children were born.

As she took the Hollywood exit to their house, she recalled the tears that were dripping from Jake's face as he helped her out of the trunk.

Jen needed to get cleaned up and out of town. How was she going to explain her bruised face to her Dad?

CHAPTER 27 - *FOLSOM PRISON BLUES.*
Johnny Cash
https://www.youtube.com/watch?v=bDktBZzQIiU

The windows in Jake's old truck were rolled down. Jake smelled Buddy's coffee before he was even out of the truck. A strange thought occurred to Jake.

If coffee tasted as good as it smelled it would be illegal.

Jake climbed out of the truck and entered Buddy's back door.

Buddy had heard Jake drive up. The old truck was noisy. He greeted Jake at his back door. It was almost daylight. The last of the bats were patrolling overhead for insects, mosquitoes mostly. The squirrels were beginning to scurry in the pecan tree in Buddy's front yard. Doves were cooing softly.

It was a perfectly normal late August morning in north Louisiana. Jake looked like a much older man these days, making him and Buddy really look like twins this morning as the men stood across the kitchen from each other.

Buddy said nothing.

He got a cup of coffee for Jake, picked up the paper and waited for Jake to speak.

Jake sat down at the table and tried to organize his thoughts. Jake was thinking *this is my problem; I don't need to get anyone else involved.*

Buddy remained quiet and returned to his paper.

Jake finally spoke. "I am in trouble."

"What did you do? Break a fingernail?" He quipped.

"No, it's a little more serious than that." He told his friend.

"Knock up some floozy? Or, maybe shoot someone?" Buddy was trying to make the point, that whatever the problem, it could be worse.

Buddy could see that Jake was not injured.

"No and Yes." At that, Buddy looked up from his paper.

Had he heard his friend correctly? Probably not.

"So, you got caught with another man's wife?" Buddy was certain that Jake had not shot anyone. Buddy knew Jake and Buddy knew that Jake only shot animals because it was good for business—Jake hated to kill anything.

"No, Buddy… I killed a man last night."

Buddy's tone was now serious, "Warm up my coffee and tell me what I can do to help you."

"I'm not sure anyone can help me." And then Jake added, "The less you know, the better."

Jen was already an accessory to murder. To his credit, Jake was having second thoughts about involving another one of the few people he truly cherished.

"Jake I can see that you need help. I can handle myself. No one will ever successfully use me as a witness against you." Buddy was savvy, he was not going in blindly; the word "successfully" was well chosen.

Killing a man is serious business. Buddy did not delude himself into thinking that more knowledge could come with no consequences. "I'm a big boy. You need help or you wouldn't be here. I can handle the consequences. You're my best friend. If I can help, I will. Tell me what happened."

"Jen has already been hurt; I don't want you hurt, too." Jake told him.

"Quit acting like a martyr, you are acting more like a titty baby than a killer. It's obvious that you aren't hurt, tell me what happened." Jake needed help. He realized that he was lucky to be alive. Buddy was the only person Jake could trust, other than Jen, and unless he came up with a plan he was going to die or go to jail or die in jail.

Jake went back to his truck and retrieved the aluminum briefcase, the rolling suitcase, the switchblade knife, the two cell phones and the three guns.

Buddy was in for an old fashion show and tell.

Jake took the items into Buddy's shop where there was more room and where Jake would be more comfortable. Jake looked at the items.

"Where is Jen? Is she alright?" Buddy asked him.

"With Joe Dixon." Buddy rolled his eyes.

"Where is the dead man?"

Jake started with the disposal of Mario.

Buddy was impressed with Jake's disposal of the body.

There would be stronger acid in the well and no towels or clothes at the camp before sunset.

Jake gave the short version of the death of Mario. As much as Jake knew that it was him or Mario he could not stand to relive the shooting.

Jake's house would be professionally sanitized by sunset.

Buddy would himself see to it that Kelley was diverted from the house.

Buddy would take Jake's truck and lead Kelley on a wild goose chase.

Buddy silently made these plans as Jake's story unfolded—and he did not share these plans with Jake.

The drugs were heroin, Buddy was certain of that fact.

Jake had no idea how he knew.

They both knew a man with more intimate knowledge of such matters if he was needed. Many varied and handy characters frequented Buddy's shop. Buddy told Jake that the gun that killed Mario was a Hi-point 9mm. Mario's guns were a Rossi 38 and the gun in Mario's boot was a Bersa 380, cheap but effective guns.

The Hi-point was destined to be melted and Buddy knew who could do the necessary tasks and he knew anyone he asked for help would be reliable and discreet. Buddy would tell them to ask no questions and to tell no one and it would happen.

It was not the first time Joe had ever had his breath knocked out, but it was the first time anyone had done so with such suddenness and skill.

Joe wanted to answer, but he could not talk. One man waited patiently while the other entered the house and took the cell phone from the young woman.

The young woman was assured that no one was going to be hurt. She was too short, too blond and too well-endowed to be Jeannette Cane. Joe regained his breath.

"She's not here. She called last night, she wanted to come here, but I told her not to." Joe cut his eyes at the blond.

"Where did she go?" one of the bikers asked.

"Her house, I guess."

"If you are lying I will send people to see you who are not as nice as me. If you call the police, I will send people who will kill you. If you are telling the truth, forget this whole thing and I will too. Understood?" Joe nodded.

The second man came out with the young woman. She had not been in a position to hear the instructions that had been given to Joe. "Explain to your young friend what just happened, please." These men had not been sent by Buddy because they were crazy. They had been sent because they were reliable and smart.

The bikers fired up their bikes and rode away. As soon as Buddy got the report, he called Jen on her cell phone. She was fine and almost to Chalmette. Buddy again learned that the simplest way is often the best. It seems that many lessons must be learned more than once. Buddy did not tell Jake that he was checking on Jen. Had Jake known all the facts he would have been particularly satisfied with the complicated way in which Buddy had handled the task.

An hour later Buddy turned into the driveway of Jake's house and pressed the garage door opener. Buddy was driving Jake's old truck.

Kelley was parked a block away, so tired that he did not see the truck when it passed by. The opening garage door caught Kelley's attention and in minutes he was alert, out of his truck, and walking purposefully toward Jake's house.

Kelley was about to get some answers—or so he thought.

He was almost to the house when Buddy backed out of the garage and sped past Kelley, headed towards Benton Road.

It was Cane—or so Kelley thought.

Kelley instinctively went for his gun but quickly realized this was a bad idea. It was now after 8:00 am and the streets were alive with people on their way to work and children on their way to school.

Kelley ran to his truck. Kelley thought he was lucky when Buddy got caught up in traffic as he tried to turn south onto Benton Road. Kelley soon had the old truck in his sights and he carefully followed the truck as it merged onto I-20 towards Shreveport. Buddy watched Kelley in his rear view mirror being careful not to lose him.

Buddy took the Spring Street exit towards downtown Shreveport, proceeded down Spring St. to Travis St. and turned west.

Kelley was several cars back but still close enough for Buddy to see him when Buddy turned into the parking lot for the building where Jake worked. Kelley concluded that Jake was going to work and arrived on the floor where Buddy had parked in Jake's reserved parking place just in time to see the man he thought was Jake enter the stairwell.

Kelley pulled into a nearby reserved parking place and raced to the stairwell.

Too late, Kelley heard a door close below.

He followed down the stairwell passing a man dressed in work clothes on his way up. Kelley did not hear the doorway above close because Buddy had closed it without making a sound and had entered a waiting white van where he would sit among the owner's tools. Buddy was almost immediately joined by a man in work clothes.

As Kelley made his way to Jake's office, the white van made its way out of the parking garage pausing only long enough for Buddy to puncture the right front tire on Kelley's Tahoe.

Kelley was pissed when his cell phone rang. The call was from his office. Kelley had been to Jake's office and had been told that Jake had called in sick.

Having just seen Jake in the parking garage, Kelley had barged past the receptionist and into Jake's private office.

The office was empty. Kelley was again told that Jake was gone and the office manager threatened to call security. Kelley agreed to leave being certain to check each office as he left and the men's room as well. When he returned to the garage, Jake's truck was still there and the right front tire on his Tahoe was flat. The call was from Kelley's office.

"Your stock broker called. He said that you need to make a trade. I didn't know you had a stock broker."

"Did he leave a number?"

"Yes, and it's on our caller ID."

"What's the number?" Kelley wrote it down and said curtly, "Run the number." He was about to hang up when the clerk added, "Where are you? Your boss has been asking. He says that some drugs are missing from the evidence room. Do you know anything about that?"

"Tell him that I'm following a lead and I don't know anything about missing drugs."

Within thirty minutes, Kelley's clerk called back. "The number your stock broker left is from one of those phones that you buy with prepaid minutes. It was bought here in Memphis. That's strange isn't it? And the boss wants you in his office this afternoon."

Kelley moved over to the inside wall of the garage. "I can't hear you, we have lost service." The phone in Tennessee went dead.

CHAPTER 29 - *POP A TOP.* Nat Stucky
https://www.youtube.com/watch?v=F-IY9ccbc8o

After show and tell, Buddy told Jake to get some rest. Jake climbed into the bed in Buddy's extra bedroom and slept soundly for the first time in days. When Jake woke up several hours later, Buddy was packing his 1995 Mercedes-Benz S-Class Turbo Diesel, one of the many vehicles Buddy owned. Buddy called the big Mercedes his road car.

"Get up. We're going on a road trip."

"Where are we going? Memphis?" Jake asked.

"No, we're going to New Orleans." Buddy was clearly enjoying the adventure, as he called it. To Jake, it was still an ordeal but a much more tolerable ordeal with Buddy in charge.

"Why are we going to New Orleans?"

"Memphis is their town they know too many people. Shreveport is our town we know too many people. We need a neutral site to make the exchange and we need lots of witnesses." Buddy had a plan. Jake didn't need any more details. It would take five or six hours to get to New Orleans. That would be ample time for Jake to learn the details.

Jake knew that they would be making an exchange. Big D and Kelley would get back their drugs and money in exchange for Jake's life.

Five hours later they checked into a suite at the Windsor Court Hotel. The room was booked in a fake name and paid for with cash from the rolling suit case. D had tried to kill Jake and who knows what Kelley had in mind. They could have all of the drugs back. Expenses were coming out of the cash. Buddy had booked a dinner reservation at August, across the street from the Windsor Court. Jake approved of the choice. August was and is one of the best restaurants in the world.

Over Old Fashions, Buddy and Jake discussed the "situation" (that's what Buddy called it).

"I don't think that Big D and Kelley are in this together and I checked. The Tennessee Highway Patrol is not looking for you. It looks to me like Kelley is in this alone." Buddy did not reveal just how he had checked, but Jake had no doubts that Buddy knew what he was talking about. Buddy always did.

Buddy had used Pinky's phone to talk to Big D and Mario's phone to talk to Kelley. Jake's phone had been turned off and left in Shreveport. They had also been careful not to use any credit cards for gas or anything else. If something went wrong, Buddy did not want to leave a trail. "I was careful not to mention to either that anyone else was involved."

"When will we make the exchange?" Jake asked.

"Tomorrow night. I need tomorrow to finalize my plan. They don't know that you're in New Orleans. I will tell them where and when tomorrow."

By the time they finished dinner it was almost 10:00 pm a typical two and a half hour New Orleans dinner. Big D or Kelley had paid for an extraordinary dinner of baked oysters, a cup of turtle soup, followed by sautéed red snapper topped with crabmeat accompanied by two bottles of Rombauer Chardonnay.

Jake was wondering if this would be his last supper, if so it could not have been better. Buddy suggested: "Let get an after-dinner drink." It was actually more of an order than a suggestion.

Fifteen minutes later they were sitting in Le' Booze on Bourbon Street. Buddy had a beer; Jake was sipping on a glass of Drambuie up.

Buddy, lost in thought for a moment, told Jake, "If you sit here long enough the whole world will pass by." And at that moment two six foot tall transvestites, one white and one black, sashayed by.

Across the street, three young girls with exaggerated breasts were arriving for the late shift at Rick's Cabaret. Off to the side two young black boys were tap dancing for tips and to top it off two well-dressed middle-aged couples were making their way down the street probably having just finished dinner at Galatoire's.

As usual Buddy was right. What a show, not all pretty, Jake thought as he observed an overweight couple pass by, both with shorts and jogging shoes, he in a wife beater shirt, and she in a tee shirt with a fanny pack.

A show like no other.

"This is the place where we will make the exchange," Buddy observed, "No one attracts attention here."

The trip to Bourbon Street had been for more than an after dinner drink. Buddy was on a reconnaissance mission. Buddy told Jake to sit tight and left the bar. A few minutes later Jake stepped outside and saw Buddy talking to the Lucky Dog vendor at the end of the block. Buddy seemed to be looking at the supplies stored in the cart.

When they left the bar and headed back to the hotel, a lone man with a guitar was singing and playing for tips. Jake was remembering that Jimmy Buffet got his start singing and playing in the quarter. The scruffy young boy was singing *Pop a Top*.

"Who wrote that song?" Jake asked.

The boy immediately replied, "Nat Stuckey."

Jake dropped a ten dollar bill into the boy's guitar case as they passed by. It was easy, Jake thought, to launder money in New Orleans.

CHAPTER 30 - *YOU ARE MY SUNSHINE.* Jimmie Davis

https://www.youtube.com/watch?v=GiRDVArEKL0

Back at the hotel Jake had tossed and turned and could not fall asleep. Jen was with her parents just a few miles away. As he lay there, he thought of the words of Jimmy Davis' huge hit. Most people probably think that it was a happy song but if you listen to the words, maybe not.

> "The other night dear, as I lay sleeping,
> I dreamed I held you in my arms,
> but when I woke dear, I was mistaken,
> and I hung my head and cried "

It was after 8:00 in the morning when Jake finally woke up. Buddy was in the kitchenette with a tray of croissants, butter, jellies, and coffee.

The TV was on, the weatherman was in a state of near hysteria, and a hurricane was brewing in the gulf.

Buddy's first words of the day, "That guy is about to have an orgasm."

The radar images of the storm did look ominous, but hurricanes and especially hurricane warnings were nothing unusual in New Orleans. It was Saturday, August 27, 2005. "If all goes as planned, we will be out of here by this time tomorrow."

Buddy had a plan.

And over a late lunch at Mandina's in Mid-City, Buddy revealed his plan. Buddy was enjoying Trout Meniere and a Bloody Mary.

Jake had lost his appetite, he was picking at his Shrimp Remoulade. His nerves were getting the best of him. After lunch, Jake listened to the calls Buddy made to Big D and Kelley. D and Kelley were to meet Jake at the corner of Bourbon and Conti at 10:15 pm.

Each had protested that they did not have enough time, but they did and Buddy was not going to allow them extra time to plan. Buddy wanted to control the meeting as if anything could be controlled on Saturday night at 10:00 pm on Bourbon Street.

It was 3:15 in the afternoon when Buddy hung up. It would take five or six hours to drive from Memphis to New Orleans. Even if one of them was able to charter a plane, it would probably take three hours.

Up to that point, Jake liked Buddy's plan.

Buddy and Jake returned to the Windsor Court to pack. They would leave as soon as the exchange was complete. The rest of the plan was not disclosed until Buddy came out of his room dressed just a little better than a homeless person. Buddy had arranged to work the Lucky Dog cart at the corner of Bourbon and Conti. The regular operator of that cart was taking a big risk, but Buddy would make it worth the risk. The Lucky Dog garage is located on Gravier Street just a few blocks from the Windsor Court. Buddy had arranged to meet the regular vendor at 6:30 pm.

He planned to himself push the cart to Bourbon Street.

To this point, Jake had gone along with everything Buddy had suggested. Buddy was having a ball and Jake was enjoying the relief of having someone else in charge.

But now, Jake balked.

"Buddy, I will not let you make the exchange. It's my problem. I appreciate everything you have done, but I am going to take over from here." He told his friend.

"Jake, I started out just to help you, but I have enjoyed the last few days more than I have enjoyed anything in years. I want to finish this." His friend said.

"No, I won't let you. Let me have those clothes." By the tone of Jake's voice and the look on Jake's face, Buddy knew that he could not win.

Jake got into the outfit complete with an old set of eyeglasses and a Saints hat with a gray ponytail hanging out the back. The red striped shirt would be worn open like a vest.

They went together to secure the cart. Buddy tried to give Jake a gun, but Jake refused. "You know that I am no good with a handgun. If I pull a gun, I will end up dead. I don't need a gun anyhow. There will be too many surveillance cameras and witnesses on Bourbon Street for anyone to pull a gun. That's why you planned for the exchange to be on Bourbon Street."

"That's true," replied Buddy. Big D and Kelley have too much to lose to risk gun play in front of cameras and hundreds of witnesses." Buddy added half joking: "Did you bring your baseball bat?"

The aluminum briefcase and the roller suitcase barely fit in the cart. If Jake sold too many Lucky Dogs, he would run out.

By 7:15 Jake was in business as a Lucky Dog vendor at the corner of Bourbon and Conti. He would be the first one there. Buddy was to meet Jake at the hotel after the exchange was complete. Buddy's plan was coming together.

Jake was thinking *this fool is going to get his life back tonight*. As soon as he got his life back, he was going to get Jen back.

Somehow.

CHAPTER 31 - *THE BATTLE OF NEW ORLEANS.* Johnny Horton
https://www.youtube.com/watch?v=VL7XS_8qgXM

Jake spent the first two hours surveying the scene. The Royal Sonesta Hotel was at his back as was Canal Street. Jake thought Big D and Kelley would most likely come from that direction. There were bars on every other corner.

The Famous Door was directly across Bourbon. It was a one-story building. The Jester was diagonally across the street. There was a balcony on the second floor of the Jester. The building on the other corner also had a balcony, but no one was on either balcony.

The Jester was in a two-story building, the other building was three stories. Jake did not see any activity in the upper floors of either building. Jake was thinking that it was a good thing Big D and Kelley had so little time. A person stationed on the upper floor of either building would have had an unobstructed line of fire. Jake wondered if people lived on those upper floors. If so they must work nights and sleep during the day. It would be too loud on Bourbon Street to sleep at night.

Bourbon Street was closed to vehicular traffic, but Conti was not. As he stood behind his Lucky Dog cart, a steady stream of cars and trucks slowly passed directly in front of Jake's position. Jake began to watch the vehicles as they approached from his left. As time passed the activity in the Quarter progressively increased. The vehicles passing by were barely moving; most of them were forced to stop for the throngs of pedestrians who were now parading up and down Bourbon Street. It was hot and humid. Jake was covered with a layer of sweat.

It was just after 10:00 when Jake saw Kelley. He was trying to look like any other tourist in jeans and a tee shirt, but the jeans were too tight and the tee shirt was too loose—but not so loose that it concealed the gun Kelley had in a holster under his left arm.

Jake might not have seen the gun had he not been looking for it.

Kelley wore a St. Louis Cardinals baseball cap. He was dressed much like the rest of the tourists except for one thing. Kelley was wearing his black patrol boots shined to perfection. It was the boots that first caught Jake's attention. Kelley was on foot. His back was towards Jake as he passed by. He appeared to be alone as he looked into the faces of the numerous people walking, standing about, and sitting in the bars. Kelley did not look at the ragged Lucky Dog salesman to his right.

Everything now moved fast.

Just as Kelley passed by Jake noticed the black Escalade halfway down Conti Street. Jake was pretty sure that the big man in the passenger seat was D. As he watched the Cadillac approach, Jake saw two vaguely familiar biker guys walk into Famous Door. The bikers seemed to ask a couple to move so that they could sit near the door.

Something caught Jake's attention from the balcony across Conti to the left side. Jake was certain that the door had been closed earlier, but it was now slightly ajar. The black Cadillac reached the corner of Conti and Bourbon. The passenger door opened and out stepped D.

Big D was dressed in his bespoke jeans, black alligator cowboy boots, and a silky white shirt half way unbuttoned with a heavy gold chain around his neck. He also wore a black blazer with a bulge on the left side. There was nothing subtle about Big D.

Across the street, Jake could see that Kelley had turned around and was now behind the Cadillac facing towards Jake. Behind Kelley, Jake could see a dark-skinned, muscular man with a bruised face, a bandaged left arm and a cast on his right arm. The man was watching Kelley's every move. Jake was somewhat surprised that Pinky was still alive. The Cadillac drove away down Conti towards the river. Big D and Kelley saw Jake at the same time. Pinky saw Jake a second later, about the same time that Kelley saw D. As Buddy had suspected, Big D and Kelley were not in this thing together.

Kelley spoke first. "I should have known that you would be here."

D had not seen Kelley, but he did recognize his *friend's* voice and turned away from Jake to look at him. "You here on official business?" He asked.

Kelley had hardly slept in days and he was about to learn once more that he was getting older and slower. Jake could clearly see Pinky now approaching Kelley from behind. Pinky had a plaster cast on his right arm and a bandaged left forearm.

It was Pinky alright, his face was badly bruised.

Before Kelley could answer, Pinky hit Kelley in the back of the head with his plaster cast. Pinky noticeably winced in pain. The blow staggered Kelley, but he did not go down. Kelley turned just in time to take a second blow from the cast in his temple.

Kelley fell backwards, hard and the back of his head slammed into the pavement. Kelley's eyes rolled up toward his forehead and he lay perfectly still. Kelley looked dead.

Big D nodded at Pinky.

Pinky picked up Kelley and propped him against the wall of the Royal Sonesta.

Kelley looked like a passed out drunk.

Pinky then turned and walked calmly down Conti towards the river.

Two young black men who had witnessed the encounter gathered around Kelley.

As far as Jake knew no one except for Jake and D really saw what had happened. Big D had to move fast. Before long someone would realize that Kelley was not just another drunk tourist.

Kelley was certain to draw a crowd, a crowd that would surely include some of New Orleans' finest.

D turned back to Jake, "So you're Jake Cane. You don't look a bit scary in that ridiculous disguise. Where are my drugs and my money?"

Jake was shaken, but he found the courage to talk, "The deal is you get the money and the drugs and then you forget I ever existed. Killing Kelley was not part of the deal."

"We don't have time to discuss this anymore. Where is my property?"

D was right, so Jake told him, "In the hot dog."

With that, D reached into his coat and pulled out a gun and shot Jake squarely in the chest. The force of the shot knocked Jake down on to the sidewalk.

D had started around the cart to get his *property* when he noticed there was no blood was pooling on Jake's chest.

A bullet proof vest?

D was not going to let this little shit stock broker get away. As the Escalade approached on Conti, Big D calmly raised his gun to shoot Jake in the head. D never got off that second shot.

Before he could, a single .22 caliber bullet entered Big D's head just above his right ear.

D fell dead in a heap to the pavement with the gun still clutched in his hand.

Hardly anyone stopped to see what had happened. It was as if this was a normal thing or a movie being filmed. Who knows what the throngs of people were thinking. No one took any particular notice when two young men in biker attire, with long hair, jeans, and blue jeans vests, helped the hot dog man to his feet nor did they notice when these men removed the man's red striped shirt and handed the shirt and a Saints hat to a man who could have been his twin.

CHAPTER 32 - *LOST HIGHWAY.*
Hank Williams

https://www.youtube.com/watch?v=lCgicPdsxxg

Jake was sore and had spit up a little blood as he and Buddy drove west on Highway 90 on their way back to Shreveport, but he was alive. The biker guys had helped Jake back to Buddy's car where he had laid in the back seat waiting for Buddy. Jake was not religious, but he was thanking God, but mostly thanking Buddy for the bulletproof vest. Buddy told Jake that Big D had shot Jake with a Taurus Judge loaded with a 410 gauge shotgun shell. Buddy wanted that gun but had left it with Big D. Buddy had also left his Ruger 10/.22 rifle in a second-floor condo overlooking Bourbon Street. It could not be traced to Buddy. Jake would replace that rifle.

It was 6:05 am on Sunday, August 28, 2005. In a few hours, Mayor Ray Nagin would issue a mandatory evacuation order for all of Orleans Parish. The next day Hurricane Katrina would devastate the city of New Orleans.

The money was back in the trunk of the big Mercedes and the drugs were in the Atchafalaya River. He and Buddy had left New Orleans at 3:00 am soon after the police had left the scene. No one had questioned Buddy as he pushed the Hot Dog cart back to the barn. The police had not done much of an investigation and there would be no follow-up. It took almost a week for the authorities in Memphis to get the decomposing body of one their outstanding citizens who had been murdered and several days before Kelley would be found. After Katrina, there was almost no police force in New Orleans and what was there were tied up with their own problems and displaced people with no habitable homes.

Jake asked Buddy, "What happened to the plan?"

Buddy was quiet in thought, "You know what Bob Burns said?"

Jake was perplexed. He never expected Buddy to quote poetry.

"Who is Bob Burns and what did he say?"

After a short pause, Buddy replied, "The Best Laid Plans of Mice and Men Often Go Awry."

The radio was on. Hank Williams was singing Leon Payne's *Lost Highway.*

The story continues.

Chapter 1 of the second book follows.

Cane's Corner

CHAPTER 1: *LET'S THINK ABOUT LIVING.* Bob Luman
https://www.youtube.com/watch?v=sLAA9ioRsQ0

He was a devoted father and husband and a serial adulterer. He was a highly respected civic leader and a murderer. He was a successful, reliable, and honest business man and in possession of well over one million dollars of contraband cash. It had taken James Caldwell "Jake" Cane more than twenty years to overcome his father's legacy and no time to ruin his own. To the world he was still a respected family man, leader and stock broker. To the wife he truly loved, he could no longer be trusted.

Many hours earlier Jake's best friend, Buddy Hawkins, had dropped Jake off at his downtown office. In addition to trading, Jake invested in oil and gas wells; he was well off by nearly all standards. A million dollars is a lot of money, but Jake did not "need" another million dollars. Especially, in hindsight, considering the trouble that accompanied the money he had found.

The brokerage firm where Jake worked was closed, but he had stopped by anyhow to open mail and catch up on paperwork. Jake was tired, too tired to simply get into his old pickup truck and go home., so he now found himself sitting at the bar of the Shreveport Club near his office reflecting on the events of the last week. Jake did not want to go home. Rather, he very much wanted to go home, but not to the empty rented house where he now stayed. No one would be waiting for Jake at his rental across the river, not even his devoted dog that was now dead and dissolving in the bottom of old water well with the man Jake had killed a few days earlier. Jake wanted to go to his real home and to his wife but that was not possible, so he sat and drank.

Three hundred miles away, New Orleans was bracing for Hurricane Katrina. Jake's in-laws had been forced to evacuate their home in Chalmette, a suburb of New Orleans, and were now safely in the million dollar home Jake and his wife Jeannette owned a few miles away from where Jake now sat. Tomorrow he would drive to Memphis for the funeral of a friend who had been murdered. Jake knew that he was likely the cause of his friend's murder. Would Jeannette go to the funeral? Would Jeanette go with him?

It was Sunday night and the few staff members left at the Shreveport Club were ready to go home; in the background, from the kitchen Jake could barely hear Bob Luman playing over a fuzzy radio. In his forty – plus years, Jake had dug himself out of holes before; he could do it again. It was time for him to stop dwelling on the past. It was time for him to start thinking about living.

ACKNOWLEDGEMENTS

I need to thank several people who helped me with this book, foremost, Dianne Turnley and Blake Martinez, who did the editing and Julie Miller who painted the cover. I also need to thank Ed Greer and Thorne Harris for advice, Barry Kuperman for his knowledge of firearms, Cindy Smith and Danielle Fauber for the cover, and finally, Kimberly Smith, for pushing me and helping me to publish.

PATRICK HENNESY

Patrick Hennessy was born in San Francisco, California and grew up in Bossier City, Louisiana. Patrick graduated from Bossier High, Louisiana Tech and LSU Law School. He is a retired lawyer, having practiced law in Louisiana for many years.

Patrick now lives and writes in his home in the South Highlands area of Shreveport, Louisiana. He and his wife enjoy traveling and spending time at their shot gun house in uptown New Orleans.